TRANSFERENCE

TRANSFERENCE

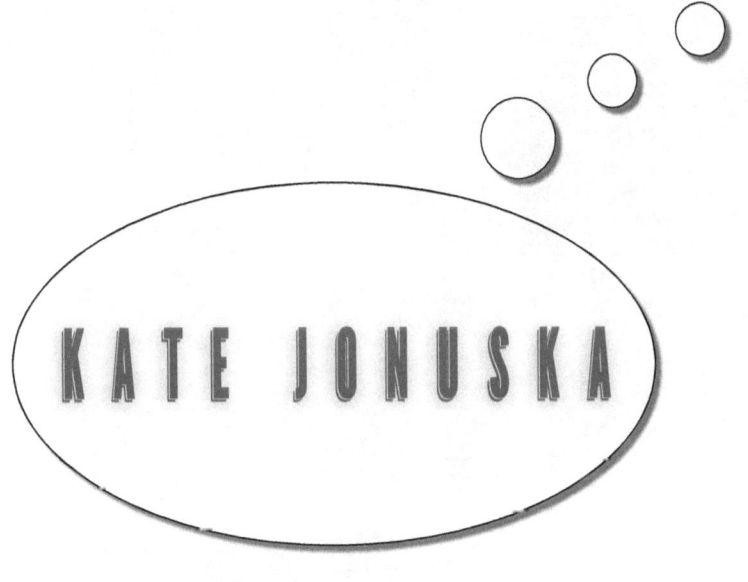

KATE JONUSKA

BKJ

We did things just how you asked
Don't try taking us to task
Didn't buy a face, no just a mask
So HAPPY HALLOWEEN!

—**"Guilty Cocker Spaniels," Modest Mouse**

1

For a mistake that ruined his life, the sex should at least have been good, but no. The orgasm that cost Dr. Derek Verbenk his job at his prestigious psychiatric practice had been mediocre at best. Seriously, he'd had better climaxes in his hand in the shower than with that patient, he lamented as, with a huff rather than a groan, he completed doing just that.

Leaning against the cold tile, Verbenk watched the water wash the emission away along with his skin's sleep-stale sweat, the perspired wine he'd consumed the night before. Despite best intentions, the slightly less tepid orgasm did little to change his mood, which was almost as black and raw as the day after his firing.

Though no one was calling it that. They'd used the phrase *mandatory resignation*. He preferred the not-untrue reframing *retirement into private practice,* and since he was determined to maintain that appearance to the world—fuck you, world—he scrupulously upkept his own. His house, his lawn, his trash bin at the curb on Tuesdays. His teeth, his nails, his facial hair, his clothes. Healthy rituals, all of them, but as Verbenk pushed his body through the motions of normality, sudsed up his chest and armpits, his mind was still gape-jawed, still obsessed, because seriously?

For a mistake that had cost him the career he'd been groomed for since birth, she should at least have been gorgeous, or at the very least, young, but no. At 40, the woman had been only a dozen years his junior, averagely pretty, wispy thin with wispy hair. She'd been single and lonely—weren't they all lonely?—but also naive and insecure and fawning, the type of woman who wanted to fill all their hollow places with validation or perhaps a man. And he was a man, wasn't he?

The steam of the shower reminded him of that overcast day. Eyes glazed, he again saw the brand of her skirt as she slipped it off her hips, saw the shoe size visible in her empty shoe. The intimacy of seeing a woman's clothing without her in it, but if anything, the memory was anti-arousing, and he didn't know why he played it on loop.

"Please," she'd said, looking at him exactly the way he liked to be looked at. And though he'd never lost control and been physically intimate with a patient before, suddenly he was deep in her hollowness while she whispered hot and muggy into his ear, "Please."

Toweling off in the safe isolation of his family mansion's master bathroom, Verbenk blushed, thinking she might still be saying "please" on his old voicemail, a phone ringing in a posh, empty high-rise office. His partners, on the other hand, had said, "blatant exploitation of transference" and "walking risk of malpractice damages" and "quietly severing the partnership to avoid fallout" and "sign the non-disclosure agreement here and here."

Malpractice. *Mal*, from the French. Bad practice, bad form, a bad boy always falling into the trap of the wrong woman. Women were just unreliable on the whole. Though this patient nonsense was new, sometimes the doctor saw his life as a parade of calamities caused by the fairer but untrustworthy sex, women who robbed a man of sense or his testicles or both at once. Women who then left as if they'd never been.

The married women (two). His college roommate's sister. The salesgirl who'd sworn she was 22. All the games of "Use or Be Used." He was only a man, and boys would be boys.

Still, yes, he admitted as he slid his dry cleaned trousers out of their plastic sheath: He should have known better as a mental-health professional, but that only made the mess worse. His grandfather, who'd founded the practice that just drop-kicked Verbenk, had studied with Freud. Doctoring the mind was what Verbenks did! Losing their shit was not, and so even as he teetered on the edge of messy, tantrum-throwing breakdown, Derek

Verbenk was determined not to be the first of his line to do so publicly.

"You will prove yourself and your worthiness anew through your thriving private practice," he told his reflection in the bathroom mirror, though perhaps *thriving* wasn't yet the right word for the new, part-time undertaking into which he was funneling his distress.

Finger-combing hair forward from his receding hairline, he knew the affirmation ritual was ridiculous, but negative self-talk and neglecting one's appearance were both sure signs of depression. After another moment meeting his own stare, he added, "You are not depressed; you are regrouping."

Verbenk hoped he made a good impression that was the case. In fact, only six weeks after hanging out his shingle—metaphorically, because the HOA would *never*—he already had a few regular patients. One of whom was due to arrive in about 15 minutes, so he buttoned his shirt across his smooth-shaved neck and went downstairs to fill his patience reservoirs with coffee.

Entering his office usually soothed him. Given the task of remodeling the previous Victorian mourning/morning room into the headquarters of his private practice, the decorator had nailed it, providing just the right set dressing for his life makeover. Bookcases lined the walls, and an overstuffed leather couch sat across from the massive desk he enjoyed roosting behind during sessions. A private side entrance off a gated courtyard offered just the right amount of patient privacy.

The appearance of the room normally charmed him back into a presentable mood, but today it wasn't enough to plug the hole inside in which the question echoed: *Seriously?* It was all so far to fall for one underwhelming fuck. You'd think he'd have learned by now—he'd tried several times over the years to swear off women completely—that fantasy was enough for him. Flesh and blood women were too risky, and fantasy hurt no one.

He'd masked himself back into professionalism by the time of his appointment. The client: Christine Blum, her third visit, one of a handful of neighborhood ladies who'd heard about his discreet practice. She lived five doors down from his house, which sat at the terminus of the cul-de-sac.

But only halfway into her session, he was already distracted. As she chatted on, instead of writing his thoughts and observations in Christine's patient notebook, Verbenk found himself tracing over the word *one*, again and again, pressing in the shape, wondering why he only saw the utter worthlessness of his long series of sexual lapses in hindsight.

"Doctor? Hello?" Christine asked from the couch, but politely, as if afraid to offend. A stunning woman, blonde and thin and out of his league, she perched on the cushions like an exotic bird, ready to take off if startled. "Are you listening?"

"Of course!" the doctor lied, vowing to try to do so from now on, even if after only a few sessions, he could tell pretty Christine was just a garden-variety Lonely. A

softball case, as were all of the thoroughly ordinary neu-
roses and crises his private practice had attracted thus
far, but Verbenk kept his goal in sight. He was proving
himself to his old partners, to the world, to himself, and so
he painted on attentiveness and said, "Please. Continue."

Christine stared for a moment, as if sizing up his
honesty.

"I'm listening," he soothed.

Lithe and elegant, she even shrugged with style.
"Maybe I've just forgotten what that feels like," said his
lovely neighbor/client, changing the cross of her legs,
which were sucked into the popular, expensive and status-
symbolic stretchy pants that seemed to pass as decent
clothing these days. Not that he was complaining.

"Well, no one around my house seems to remember
I exist lately. My husband or my son," she continued.
"Sometimes I go an entire day without speaking, because
when I do, I might as well be talking to myself, you know?
Though what a cliché that is! My problems must seem
so small in the scope of everything people go through.
Cancer, poverty, terrorism."

Though he kindly shook his head in commiseration,
Verbenk understood what she meant, knew her type.
He'd been surrounded by that milieu most of his life.
Lost in paradise, swamped with first-world problems. He
guessed she was likely the kind of bored woman who followed around her leashed dog, watching carefully for the
moment its ass would iris open and give her something
to do, something to tidy, and then wondered why she felt

unfulfilled. The type who, given every material thing, would either nag her feelings out or drown them in wine, because in the circles of this gated neighborhood, it was never problem drinking if it was just wine. Idle hands will get manicures but often need professional help to find meaning.

Still, a man needed to make a living, needed to make an impression.

"Here's another cliche," Christine said. "No one would notice if I just disappeared. I suppose we all think that sometimes. I'm sure you hear that all the time."

Her gaze danced over his face, as if for confirmation.

"It is a common feeling, certainly, but let me assure you, you would be missed," Verbenk recited, but he was actually still focused on her pants. Slim legs, long and lean, but thankfully topped with womanly hips. A great, athletic body and youthfully long blonde hair, rare in a woman her—their—age.

"Tell me more about when you feel that way," he said, "when you feel..."

"Invisible?" she supplied.

"Invisible," he agreed, though he'd no idea how a woman this beautiful could be invisible, edging past 50 or not. She was very visible to him because despite his best intentions at full attention, Verbenk was picturing her naked. Specifically, her ass. It would be shapely and firm thanks to her bi-weekly cross-pumped, pi-yo-spinning or whatever the ladies did nowadays, but with enough flesh to still give a healthy jiggle.

He blushed slightly at his naughtiness—fantasy hurt no one—but *that* kind of hindsight, he'd always been good at that. It was a gift.

She said, "Well, when you're not heard, it's easy to feel you're not seen, too, you know? Just the other day, I..."

And then she was off and running with a summary of her latest boilerplate midlife-crisis stories. Angst over her teenaged son switching colleges, then an argument about her banker husband taking a new promotion—and the fancy new car he'd bought with the promotion money. Both issues were obviously wallpaper over an empty-nest identity issue, which would not be solved by denying her husband a mid-life sports car. In this neighborhood, a mid-life convertible was *de rigueur* for a man in his 50s.

An age Verbenk was, too. At 52, he should have been at the top of his game. Serious and powerful and authoritative by virtue of a bit, but not too much, gray hair. His 50s were where a man became The Man. At least, such had always been the unspoken promise, that life would flower at a certain point, and Verbenk felt cheated. He thought he'd have it figured out by now. He was still mostly slender, the kind of man who went stringy with age except for the belly, but he'd grown up and grown calcified into nothing special. Suddenly, he was in his own fantasy with Christine. Her ass and his stomach, her healthy jiggle and his horrifying one, his aging skin sloshing like custard.

Blinking rapidly to clear the vision, the doctor nodded and mm-hmmed at the points Christine seemed to expect it, while he mused.

Idea: We notice the jiggle of the superficial skin without understanding the workings of the meat beneath; we notice only the consequences of our actions without understanding why we act in the first place. This was the kind of psychiatric exercise Verbenk found enthralling, the murky territory where the sub- and unconscious clashed, where wars were fought for human souls. But today the flesh-driven metaphor felt too personal, because while exploration of behavior and motivation was supposed to be his job, he still didn't understand why he'd fucked that patient. He didn't understand his own meat.

Distracted yet again, he was back in that stormy day. His patient's mouth fumbling on his bare shoulder, the rug burn on his knee from his stumble while—for lack of a more flattering term—dismounting. The real thing never resembled porn, did it?

"Dave doesn't approve of therapy, you know," Christine was saying. "I haven't told him."

Dave? Right! The husband. Verbenk refocused. His mistake was past, and this woman was present. He was a psychiatrist, and he was determined to prove he was still a good one. Even if the road to redemption was paved with housewives.

"Why didn't you tell him?" he asked. "Or rather, why don't you want to tell him?"

Christine sighed, which made her lovely bust rise and fall. "Why do I need anything else when he gives me everything?" she asked, the phrase ringing like repeated words. The husband's words on her tongue, Verbenk guessed.

"After all, if I can't be happy where I am, surrounded by everything a person might want, maybe I'm just too stupid to be happy. Maybe I'm just old and broken."

The doctor frowned. Not according to her ass! But he remained quiet, watching her body language. "Oh? What makes you think that?" he asked, then allowed a silent spell to stretch, to pull out vital details, as silence always did.

"I used to model, you know," Christine finally said. Her arms were crossed, her frame so graceful. "But now I have the perspective of... a certain age. Youth and beauty, they're..." She faded out, only to come back with more energy and volume than she'd projected all day. "Did you know I had this done?" she asked, tapping her nose with a finger. Thin lines wrinkled around her eyes as she smiled ironically.

The doctor shook his head. The nose was quite nice, beautifully bland, as if airbrushed.

"I sometimes wish they would have just cut it off," she said with surprising violence, her hands falling, balling into fists on her knees. Verbenk didn't move, breathing quietly, a spectator watching her thought process.

She quickly recovered, though, again sitting upright with the posture of a former runway walker. As if leaning back into the cushioned leather was a sign of weakness.

"I sometimes think: If I didn't model, I would have been forced to have something more than looks, you know? I'd have been forced to be something more?" she asked, making her statements into tentative questions, as if waiting for Verbenk's ruling on her feelings. "To be something other than pretty and a long time ago? Like, if I was ugly, I'd be allowed to be unhappy?"

Verbenk leaned forward, elbows on the desk's calendar blotter. Three months since the incident, he couldn't help but note, but he was determined to not to be sidetracked.

"So you wish you didn't get what you wanted in life? You wish you'd wanted different things?" he asked, secretly incredulous. "Is that what you're saying?"

Mixed-up woman. She was right that she had it good, and maybe she just needed permission to start enjoying it. Maybe she should buy *herself* a sports car. Or whatever rich women did instead around that age. Begin an affair with the pool boy?

Christine admitted, "Talking about my unhappiness always sounds so stupid when I say it out loud." He opened his mouth to advise, but she cut him off, with a suddenly sunny disposition. "Gratitude. I know. Hashtag blessed and shit." Christine colored at her use of profanity.

He suppressed a snort. An attitude of gratitude. He'd seen that embroidered once on a pillow, and Verbenk found himself smiling wanly, too, because how precious these normal little problems were. Pillows could do this new job of his.

A case of angst. This woman obviously craved a new direction, purpose or project, a way of embracing her life's next stage—and this time not including plastic surgery, he hoped, because she wasn't that age-ravaged just yet.

"These confused feelings, let me assure you, are very normal, especially when you reach…" How had she put it?

" . . . a certain age. Anxiety and discontent of this sort are often manifestations of dissonance between who we are and who we want to be, between where we are and where we yearn to be."

She sniffed. "I'm sure you're right."

"Usually a shift in routine or perspective is helpful," he said. "Opening yourself up to the next chapter of yourself. Often this takes the form or a new job, a new skill, an old hobby, a new hobby. Even if the effort at first seems superficial, the rewards can be immense."

With a lift of one shoulder, she said, "I have been known to do some art. Drawing and painting and—"

"Lovely!" he enthused. "Might be just the thing."

Christine smiled weakly and smoothed her hair back into its ponytail. Such a feminine gesture. His heart melted a bit, and then his professional guard slammed back down with a medieval clang.

No. He'd not get snared again. Female loneliness had a gravitational quality that could suck you in and obliterate a man's sense. Oh, the *needs.* Consulting the clock—12:50 p.m.—he closed her patient notebook.

"Next session, let's talk a bit about relaxing into the present and giving yourself permission to be happy, shall we?" he asked, cheerfully extricating himself from her life's foibles. "Our time is up for today."

The doctor stood, but Christine failed to follow. Instead she gazed down, chin tilted, the picture of innocence. *Ah,* he thought, planting his hands on the desk and waiting.

A doorknob moment, when a patient kept for last what really troubled, what they really wanted. He could tell by the opening and quick closing of her mouth, there lay a meaty issue, a deep and unnamable need.

"Christine?" he asked. He could not help her if she could not communicate.

She shrugged, embarrassed, her hands on her knees. "The Xanax?" she said. "I need a refill."

Suppressing a sigh, Verbenk reached for his prescription pad. It had been less than three weeks since he'd prescribed a month's supply, but it was a low dose, with a little room for harmless abuse. Maybe drugs were simply the best remedy for the female Lonely. Besides, he had little desire to judge what got her through, because with no more patients on the schedule, his thoughts turned instantly to the open bottle of wine in the fridge from last night. It wasn't problem drinking if it was wine and after the workday. He wasn't drinking two whole bottles himself a night yet or anything.

The word *yet* in his head made Verbenk cringe. Such negative thinking. He would feel slightly off until he could get to a mirror and reset himself with his affirmations.

Buzzing with nerves, Christine stood as he wrote out the script. He saw her cheeks and shoulders relax when she held the paper between her fingers. Softball case, indeed. Only an illegible signature necessary.

"Thanks, Dr. Verbenk," Christine said with genuine emotion. She handed over his payment in cash—another

way she was keeping the session from her husband, Verbenk now realized—and allowed him to lead her to the
door and shut it behind her.

This work used to be a joy. Derek Verbenk perhaps
didn't have the illustrious career of either his grandfather, Chester Verbenk, or his uncle, Sherman Verbenk.
Both were widely published and esteemed, and had been
popular guest speakers, striding back and forth with
vests straining at the buttons with integrity in front of
high-profile audiences. Uncle Sherman had also been a
prized expert witness in cases of murder and/or mania.
The highest notoriety Derek himself had achieved was an
award for his early work with Eye Movement Desensiti-
zation and Reprocessing for severe cases of PTSD. In the
late 1990s. Now everyone did EMDR and no one cared.

But the consolation for lack of prestige had always been
that, before the work had turned on him, he'd genuinely
enjoyed the job. He'd loved psychiatry as a science, a road-
map as complicated yet logical as the branching anatomy
of the human brain, but a map nonetheless. There was
comfort to be found in the idea that human neurons must
have once appeared magical—an entire consciousness
created from electrical signals—but science and rigor had
begun to unlock their secrets.

"Psychiatry is the owner's manual of the human experience," his uncle had been fond of saying. "We tame
demons. We shine light into the darkness and make sense
of chaos, and so can you, if you have the wits and strength,
boy."

He'd been in high school at the time, and his uncle had found him crying over some emotional melodrama that the older man found facile and ridiculous. When you understood the human mind as a doctor did, his uncle intimated, emotions were child's play to control.

"You're a young man now," Sherman had said, "and you're a Verbenk. We are men of science. Pull it together and don't be an embarrassment." *Like your mother* was left unsaid.

Right. *Pull yourself together.*

Now as he shut the door on Christine's pretty but unchallenging ass, the doctor feared he'd never get an interesting case again. The former model was the fourth neighborhood woman for whom he was prescribing, and he guessed most of the others' husbands were also in the dark. If that number continued to increase, he should just leave a pad of signed scripts for Xanax and Valium and Adderall—the housewife trifecta—outside the door with the patient's name left blank. Perhaps an honor-system slot in the door for payment.

If everything were as pointless as that, though, the doctor might as well ditch all his positive thinking and bolstering routines and hygiene and alcohol monitoring. Take some time off to really fall apart and engage with some of his own meaty issues, like: Had he ever earned his position at the practice, or was his entire career pity- and/or nepotism-based?

He recoiled at that idea, because doctors were the fixers, not the broken, and he couldn't let them know, couldn't let them see. The idea of real retirement with hours and hours of time for gazing and falling into his navel—and what he might find there—scared the shit out of Verbenk. Once again, he pressed back the tide of breakdown.

He'd taken only one stride toward the kitchen and his good-job-done glass of wine when an unexpected knock sounded on the patient door. The knock itself was unusual; Christine and most his other clients knew to press the intercom buzzer, which could be heard from throughout the house. Turning back, through the peephole he saw a woman with a strawberry-blonde bob of hair. She wore a fitted blue sweater and dark, stylish jeans, the kind that cost three figures. The kind that usually made women's asses look amazing. Artsy turquoise jewelry hung around her neck.

Still spying, he saw the woman roll her deep-brown eyes and he pulled back, wondering what made her so impatient. Verbenk opened the door only a few inches, leaving her for the moment standing on the patio next to three lovely, blooming rose bushes. The gardener's work, which along with the maid's, had always done the necessary job of making it appear that he had his shit together.

"Yes? May I help you?" he asked, hoping he couldn't, because dammit, he'd already done something today.

"I certainly hope you can." The woman had her fingers woven together over her flat, fit stomach, the posture of a soloist or a public speaker, someone used to commanding attention. She nodded her head once, as if confirming this fact.

Dr. Verbenk was one part intimidated by her manner and one part aroused. Purely fantasy, purely amusement, of course, but since he'd recently had such bad sexual results with a submissive woman, maybe a confident and powerful one...

"But you are making me seriously uncomfortable right now," said his visitor, grimacing and looking over her shoulder toward the street. "I don't know if I can do this."

Verbenk immediately shelved his irritation at her interruption and opened the door wide, embarrassed that he'd selfishly neglected patient privacy and kept her waiting. "Seeking therapy can be a hard step," he said, aiming for a tone of gracious wisdom, "but it's also a brave one. Please, come in."

Another housewife. He just knew it, but *proving himself*, and all.

Her step into his office was nervous, but her annoyed manner indicated she was unaccustomed to such timidity. She didn't like not being in charge. As she slipped past him, he got a closer look at her pretty face, which seemed vaguely familiar. Late 20s or a year past 30 at most, he gauged. Such a great, ripe age for a woman. Verbenk also noted with pleasure that he was right about the jeans as she walked further into the room. Spectacular denim.

He revised his estimate. Not a musician. Too clean-cut, too much of the cheerleader/fundraiser in her. Definitely an establishment chick: pretty, but uptight and predictable. Probably went straight from being president of a university sorority to president of the Junior League or something. Probably worked in some bullshit industry like public relations or marketing. Shapely hindquarters, though, which was a bonus even if she turned out to be just another Lonely, just another prescription hound.

"I'm not lonely," said the woman, crossing her arms and quickening her pace toward the patient couch.

Verbenk started at her prescience, then shook his head, striding toward his desk and the authority its bulk always supplied him. "Well, if your name is not Lonely," he joked, "perhaps you'd like to sit down and tell me what it actually is."

"Great. A dad joke." She huffed onto the leather sofa, so recently vacated by another female ass. He pictured both side by side in his mind, mentally comparing—the women and the butts. Both lovely, if different flavors of lovely. "My name is Janet," she said, "and dear God, you're repulsive. You know that? No wonder that other woman doesn't trust you."

The doctor's mouth fell open. "Excuse me?" He had no idea what he'd done in the last 60 seconds to offend other than harmlessly fantasize.

"Oh, don't worry. She hates me, too," the woman mumbled, her shiny hair brushing her cheeks as she shook her head. "But that's none of my business. I never wanted it to be my business. I just want… never mind."

Some barely cloaked anger there. More husband issues? Yes, there was indeed a wedding ring on her left hand. Sliding open a drawer, Verbenk removed a new notebook—an old Verbenk tradition he'd upheld despite convention. The label for a new patient's name was blank on its cover. Another new client would be another checkmark for productivity, another day with head above water. Despite the missed wine in the fridge, he actually welcomed it. The woman seemed interesting.

He asked, "So what brings you to my door today?"

Diamond studs sparkled in her ears. The planes of her face were lovely, if somewhat generically so, everything symmetrical, though a more careful examination revealed a little tired under her eyes. Almost in answer, she closed those eyes for a moment too long to be a blink, then sighed.

"Valium," she answered, meeting his gaze and again weaving her fingers together, prim and controlled. "I can't relax, and I'm told that you dole out that kind of thing with minimal fuss."

How uncouth! Though drugs were a typical goal in this business, most clients were more roundabout in their approach, and Verbenk bristled. He'd need to find out just to whom she'd spoken—after this Janet woman officially became a client, thereby thriving up his practice.

"I assume you're experiencing anxiety, then," he said, falling back on the platitudes that over the years he'd learned worked best on un-psychiatric-educated minds.

"We all experience it to varying degrees during different periods. What might have brought this on? Are you finding yourself troubled by specific events or thoughts?"

"Funny. It's not *my* thoughts that are the problem," said Janet, laughing ruefully, then pressing her lips together. "My issue is rather difficult to explain, so I am going to shoot from the hip: Yes, I came for the drugs. I know what I need, I'm very busy, and questions seem like a waste of my time and yours."

Verbenk squinted at that idea, saying, "Questions are what therapy is all about."

This time, the eye roll was unmistakable—and expert, making him feel like a school boy, even though he'd been in medical school when this girl was in diapers.

"No, no, no," Janet said emphatically. "I don't want to go through actual therapy. I'm too exhausted for therapy." To the doctor's surprise, her poise crumbled, as did her composure. "I just want the thoughts to stop, not to *talk* about them, don't you see? It's just not fair. Just a few weeks ago, bang, these thoughts. I wasn't prepared to deal with... this, let alone *talk* about it. It's too..."

As she spoke, Janet slumped over, finally coming to lay across the couch like a patient in a cartoon, going from full self-possession to feet-on-the-furniture comfort like zero-to-sixty. Women were so damn mercurial. The action did, however, allow him to take stock of her boots for the first time. Heeled and black, hugging over her jeans up to the knee. Hot.

"Are therapists supposed to think about their clients' hotness, or are you just a creep?" she asked.

Honestly spooked, "Where did that...? What exactly are you saying here?" he asked, trying to smooth down his nerves. "Let me assure you, not only is this a safe and confidential space, but I've heard it all. Whatever is bothering you, I promise you cannot shock me."

Janet sat up again, her face skeptical. She took the throw pillow with her, hugging it to her breasts for comfort or as if to block his view. He hadn't thought he'd been staring at her chest, but wasn't sure. She said, "You'll think I'm crazy."

"We don't like that word, generally," he said, leaning back and crossing his legs, knowing he held the prescription pad and therefore the power, "but why don't you try me?"

"So you're going to be like that?" she demanded. "No talk, no drugs?"

Verbenk nodded. "I am."

She answered with an angry, growling sigh. "Fine. Fine, I can do this. I'm... The problem is that I'm..." But then silence followed. He let it stretch, but the quiet refused to do its work. She opened her mouth several times, only to close it and reposition her hands.

"Janet?" he prompted, speaking her name for the first time. For a moment, he thought she was staring past him, over his shoulder, perhaps at the titles of the books his decorator had chosen for his shelves to make him look learned and trustworthy. He'd never opened a one of them.

"I'm..." she began, and then required one more swallow. "I've become telepathic." The last word was spit out with distaste.

Verbenk was momentarily speechless himself. *Well, then.* Apparently he had *not* heard it all. Even worse, apparently her prescience wasn't all in his head.

But the doctor turned firmly toward dismissive: No way. There was no way. Something as ridiculous as a belief in telepathy was abnormal psychology territory, where dwelt delusions of grandeur, alien abductions, and people who believed themselves time travelers sent back to kill Hitler. Psychiatry did not cover mind-reading or magic, nor the ability to move objects with their minds, like a poltergeist or a Jedi. Pure fantasy.

"No, that's telekinesis," said Janet, and a shock ran through Verbenk, because this time she'd answered his thought directly. "Oh, I've done my research on supernatural abilities the last few weeks," she continued, her tone exhausted. "And I don't have the Force. Just the ability to read minds and feel other people's emotions. Sadly."

He was too surprised to laugh aloud. This was serious. She was in his head. Stunned, Verbenk fell back on the technique of turning the last word of a patient's sentence into a question, saying, "Sadly?"

"Yes, sadly, because would you want to read what was on your mind, Dr. Verbenk?" she asked.

His eyes flicked down to the pillow in front of her chest, which Janet only gripped tighter. The doctor's heart began to race as he looked honestly at the thoughts he'd had so far that day. Christine's naked ass, jiggling. Afternoon wine and shower masturbation and… self-doubt, which he'd always been taught to keep hidden at all cost. The rain on his former office's window and the patient's dry lips, the voicemail "pleases."

"Oh, great," said Janet, flinging herself back into the cushioned leather, the pillow held like an airplane's cushion floatation device in her arms. "With a patient? In your office, even? So that's why you're hidden away like this. I should have known the reason would be tawdry. It always is."

No. Verbenk ran his fingers through his thinning hair, unconsciously shaking his head in disagreement, because this woman he'd just met could not know his biggest secret about his worst fuck-up, snap, just like that. Like catching a cold, catching a secret. *No.*

He fumbled for other explanations. Maybe this Janet person was good at interpreting body language or expression, as some people were. Maybe despite the nondisclosure agreement, she knew someone who knew someone who'd said something—

"The client's name was Sandra, if you need further proof," Janet said, slumping back to horizontal as if under the weight of his past. "Don't make me describe what she was wearing."

Janet was right, but... *No!* It wasn't possible. Either Verbenk was delusional or Janet was, and since he was the doctor, she was the obvious choice. Risperdal then, he thought, maybe some old-fashioned Haldol. A good anti-psychotic, that was the answer, and there was no need for this cold fear flooding his belly. He'd prescribe some meds and work his therapy magic and this woman would become a long-term patient, just another nut in another grand old family's tree. People in neighborhoods like this one were good at cultivating and hiding away their nuts. Upperclass tradition, really.

"So you *do* believe in crazy," Janet replied. "Shit. I know that I can't just pretend it's not happening anymore, hoping it will just go away or that I'll wake up from this nightmare, but I shouldn't have come here." Staring at the ceiling, she muttered, "There's no help here."

Verbenk stared at his new patient's face, scanning it for truths. "Wait," he said, a thought crackling like lightning. "I know you, don't I? You're..."

My Senator's wife! His Senator's hot, almost-inappropriately younger wife. Janet Buckmann was her name. She'd made national news back in 2012 for helping "invigorate" the campaign of her husband Senator Orin Buckmann, who'd spent several terms languishing in the State Senate before finally making the leap to D.C. And that was right. He'd heard that like Verbenk, the Senator lived in Cherry Creek—when he wasn't in Washington, that is.

He remembered one of the ads during his last campaign. Or rather, a specific scene from one ad in which

Janet wore a tight white T-shirt with the campaign logo and was reading to a group of children of color at a rec center. Liberal heartstrings stuff—she was supposedly a "philanthropist" as her "job," but really? A politician's wife was perhaps the paragon of all housewives.

"Oh, shut up and take the air quotes off my philanthropy, asshole, though I really wish you didn't know who I am," said Janet, rocking slightly back and forth, words rapid-fire. "I just need it to stop, you see, just long enough to figure this out and keep all my balls in the—"

Two steps behind her train of thought, he stated, "You're Janet Buckmann."

"We covered that, didn't we?"

Still, he hoped it wasn't true, prayed it wasn't real. "I didn't say aloud that I knew who—"

"You didn't have to." She snapped her fingers. "Now keep up."

Fuck, Verbenk thought, and he discovered he was convinced. He'd met a woman who could read his mind. The implications of that reality then hit, sending adrenaline rippling through his body. His face flushed hot. Verbenk's heart beat in his ears. *Thud. Thud.*

All his mouth managed to say was a long, breathy, "Fuuuuck," but his brain went into overdrive, instinctively listing all the other things he *shouldn't* think about it front of this woman, which only succeeded in producing a memory parade of all the worst things he'd done in his life. Telling his first girlfriend—a vapid, trusting girl—that he loved her in order to get that last button undone.

Bribing a journal to publish his papers back in the 80s. Furtive sex in a parked car outside the memorial service for his Uncle Sherman, the man who'd raised him and led him into the profession. That woman had left him, too, not two weeks later.

All that in the space of *thud, thud, thud*. Images spun up and down and round like a carousel in his gray matter, but it was Janet who seemed to get motion sick. His new patient sprang to her feet in obvious distress and paced in front of the couch. She held her hands like bookends to her temples.

"Horrible, horrible," she muttered. "Negative emotions especially make me physically ill. Stop it!"

"OK," he said, frozen, commanding his traitorous thoughts away, but he couldn't. The slideshow continued against his will.

Backing over his neighbor's barky little dog with his car in his driveway; using a snow shovel, he'd moved the body into the street to avoid both blame and the necessity of delivering bad news. The fake phone numbers he'd left on dressers rather than take on the complications of the woman still sleeping.

Verbenk wanted to slam his forehead against the desk to make the readable thoughts stop. Mind reading was the plot of a comic book, the kind his mother used to buy him as a young boy when it had just been the two of them. The kind he'd read to tatters but his uncle had later confiscated, saying, "The sooner you realize this is not how the world works, the better." All that fantastical stuff was best left behind, along with his mother's bohemian, transitory lifestyle.

Before Janet had arrived, he'd already been so close to the edge of breakdown that now he felt the chaos looming and heavy. His fingers were trembling.

"Stop feeling sorry for yourself and help me," Janet pled, still pacing in her heeled boots, her hands now clutching her stomach. "This is not a comic book. I'm a real person."

The doctor jumped to his feet, raising his voice. "If this is going to work, you will have to let me speak my thoughts every once in a while before answering them!" He panted slightly with the exertion of the words.

She snapped to attention with fists at her hips, equally frustrated. "If this is going to work, you will have to stop panicking."

He shouted, "I am not panicking!"

But of course, he was. His vision was too bright, too crisp, sickening. Barely keeping his feet, Verbenk leaned heavily against the desk. Goosebumps prickled his legs, and he felt his testicles shrivel up to his body in mortification. Yep, that was panic. She'd diagnosed him before he had.

Mal practice. Bad doctor. Bad man.

"Stoooooop," she whined. "I'm like a sponge for thought. It's… it's overwhelming." Her fingers flexed into claws, her words spilling faster. "I mean, I see my husband's dreams while he's asleep, and if I can get through that, thoughts sometimes seep in from passing cars. You ever wonder what people are doing and thinking at 3 a.m.? Ever wonder what the parent of the screaming toddler at the mall really wants to do to him? People are horrible. Horrible. Trust me."

Oh, Verbenk knew he was horrible. After all, he'd been stuck in that regrettable, forbidden moment of sexual transgression for months.

"A literal dirty old man." Janet's pacing sped up, as did her breathing. "You. Are. Reprehensible. It's like... I'm dissolving... and... dizzy..."

She flapped her hands at the wrists, eyes squeezed shut as if waiting for a contraction to pass. Not that she'd had kids yet, he saw, looking at her hips. *Stop it! She can hear you!*

"I can hear *everything!*" The woman's skin, which was red-head pale, became red as a balloon. She must have been holding her breath. She wavered off-balance. Janet was going to pass out.

The medical doctor inside Verbenk leapt into action. He shot up from his chair and around the desk to grip her by her slender shoulders, firm but not violent. She shook between his hands, her knees weak.

"Breathe." He wasn't usually good with hysterics, but Verbenk felt as if he'd caused this. His thoughts had done this, had poisoned her system, and now it was his responsibility to calm her down. And so, "Calm down," he said, too loud.

"You're still panicking!" she accused, taking in a lungful of air. "*You* calm down!"

Always a man to prefer method over madness, Verbenk hunted through his brain for emergency soothing techniques and came up with a handful, top of which was—

"Don't you dare slap me," she warned, violently pointing an index finger in his face.

He didn't have any injectable sedatives at the home office, either. "What about thinking of a happy place?" Verbenk suggested weakly.

Obviously still distressed, Janet curled her lip in derision. "A fucking happy place?" she growled, her gestures becoming wild. "I've had this more than three weeks. Like I haven't tried a fucking happy place?!"

Jesus, it was refreshing to hear a woman swear like a normal person. To toss four-lettered truth bombs. To really lose her shit instead of attempting to hold it together with support hose and super glue, like so many women he'd seen over the years seemed to think was normal.

"But I NEED to hold it together, understand?" The whites of her eyes were lit with manic fire, though her body looked like it would crumble into dust if he let her shoulders go. "That's why I came here. I can't do this myself!" She struggled for breath, choking on the words. "You! You must do something. Help me, or I'll... tell someone about Sandra. Don't think I won't."

Low blow.

"Fine," he snapped back. He steered Janet bodily back to the couch, urged her to sit and knelt in front of her slender knees. One was bouncing in anxiety, the low heel of her boot tapping the carpet at hummingbird-wing speed.

Drastic times, drastic measures, even if those measures were hippy-dippy. If she could "absorb," as she said, awful thoughts, certainly she could absorb calming ones, even if that meant he had to, too.

Leaning back onto his heels at her feet, his knees cracking, Verbenk cleared his head of thoughts, picturing an eraser wiping a white board. He'd meditated exactly once, decades ago in college, while drunk no less, and he'd felt more like a sack of shit at the end of the attempt than its beginning. Guided meditation, he'd always thought, was for minds simpler than his—or people braver—but he nonetheless remembered a few techniques.

Janet shot him a skeptical look, but seemed incapable of speech, perhaps needing all her energy just to breathe.

The beach. He imagined waves crashing on a generic, white-sanded beach below a sky of crystalline blue. Palm trees, identical and almost cartoonish. Verbenk concentrated on the warmth of the sand beneath his body, on visualizing the tiny bubbles dancing in the retreating waves, something so delicate surviving in something so big and strong. The image began to gain depth.

The sea retreated. That was the exhale of the guided meditation, picturing the water shushing out into the depths as the breath did. Then his inhale drew the waves back up the beach like a magnet, held for a moment at the highest point on the sand and the fullest lungs, then again the shush of pushing the water out. Rise and fall of the chest, rise and fall of the ocean. Shush in, shush out. Everything in control. Verbenk could almost feel the tug of the tide on his feet, the slow work of the waves undermining the grains of sand beneath him.

Cracking an eye, he checked to see if the exercise was working the way he'd hoped. Janet's eyes were shut and her face had relaxed. This close, the doctor could see the delicate wrinkles around her eyes, adorable hints at the crow's feet that would annoy her in 10-15 years. Such a poor, young thing. Janet's lip began to curl again, so he snapped the thought away and shut his eyes.

He concentrated again on pushing the water, controlling waves with the power of the moon, with the power of his breath. To his white-sand beach, he added a little boy. Himself as a child with a plastic bucket and shovel, patting together a sand castle and humming happily. Just the humming and the waves.

The book-lined office was intensely silent as they sat this way for minutes, 10 minutes, then 15 and longer, for as long as he could sustain the image in his mind. The castle grew four towers, the child's fingers working hard to get the crenellations along the battlements just right. The tide continuing to breathe.

Finally, "OK," she said. "Thank you."

Verbenk was so deep in the exercise that his first uneven inhale outside the vision felt awkward and wrong, and he was lightheaded, like a man performing mouth-to-mouth who preserves too little oxygen for himself.

"That will do, I suppose," said Janet, breathy but sure. The doctor regained focus to find his newest client perched above him on the couch, elbows on knees and chin on palms, rather calmly surveying him. Put together again, it seemed. This demeanor, he intuited, this was the real Janet Buckmann, not the frazzled creature who'd walked in. She continued, "I suppose you're not *so* shitty a human being that I won't accept a prescription from you. I'd rather not go through all this again with a different doctor."

Valium. Right. He had no reservations about granting the prescription now. Verbenk's knees cracked once more as he regained his feet. Legs on pins and needles, he leaned on the furniture to get back to his desk. He'd get his prescription pad and he'd get her that Valium and he'd get her the hell out of his office so he could figure out what the fuck just happened.

As soon as the thought occurred, Janet stood, walked to the desk and grabbed his prescription pad, shoving it into his hands. "10 milligrams, I think," she said. Before he could express his question, she explained, "I can Google. Just some Valium. I'll be fine. They're just thoughts, right?"

Falling into his chair, feeling like a tube of squeezed toothpaste, the doctor scribbled out the dosage and his signature. He felt dissected, as if she'd ripped him open and put what were supposed to be indoor organs on the outside of his body. He felt... so very much, all his buried bodies surfacing, and he didn't like that, had never liked that. Feeling things.

Wine. He needed the wine. And he needed the person with this scary, discomfiting ability away from him. Now.

"Poor you." Janet snatched the prescription out of his hands. "Try *having* the ability sometime."

Then without asking his rates, she counted out several bills and laid them on his desk. Eyes locked blurrily on the money, Verbenk heard her boots cross the carpet, and looked up only when she cleared her throat.

Holding up one authoritative finger, Janet said, "You'll say nothing of this to anyone."

Verbenk was unable to shake his head fast enough in agreement.

Finger still extended, "And you will never think about me when you're in the shower."

"No," he whispered, his face wincing closed in embarrassment.

"I'll be fine," she repeated, turning again to leave. "I'll be fine."

2

*H*e tried. Three weeks later, squirming in the wing chair he'd pulled out from its decorative corner for his fourth session with Janet Buckmann, Dr. Derek Verbenk closed his eyes and truly tried to concentrate. He pushed his mind until he could swear his brainstem ached in the tender, vulnerable spot where head met neck, but the ocean wouldn't come. His energy flickered moments into the meditation, and he ground his teeth together in frustration.

"Take a few minutes and try again," said Janet from the couch, where she'd flounced down 10 minutes late for their 1:30 appointment, shaking the massive Starbucks to-go cup in her hand as an excuse. Now the coffee sat on the carpet in reaching distance beside her black REI-chic shoes on his Persian carpet, and she'd fallen into what was becoming her habitual position: head upon a pillow on one side of the sofa, ankles crossed on the other. She settled her shoulders more comfortably, eyes closed, and said, "I'll wait right here."

Verbenk's fingers gripped the wooden chair arms tighter, both insulted at her tone and disappointed in himself. This afternoon the meditative ocean felt as far away as the actual ocean, which in Denver, meant as far as it was possible to get. Leading her in that practice—an unfamiliar and draining technique he'd never before used—had begun to feel like transferring energy into a leaky bucket.

And if the bucket could please keep her voice down, he thought in Janet's direction as he massaged his pounding forehead, *that would be much appreciated.*

It wasn't the best day. Prescription-strength ibuprofen was barely keeping his hangover from last night at bay, but he'd needed the wine to fend off the dreams. Transparent dreams, all forgotten clothing and cracking glass walls, and in between, spells spent watching his own awful thoughts and memories parade across the blank canvas of his bedroom ceiling at 3 a.m. Since Janet had entered his life, her case had taken it over. Even alone, he'd felt spotlighted. "Come one, come all, and see the slimiest creature ever to crawl from the earth's depths and pass the boards," the sideshow barker in his head shouted. In fact, it had been three weeks now of this constant, shouting self-awareness. He'd finally fallen asleep only a few hours ago and was having trouble shoring up the mental defenses necessary to spar with Janet.

"Meditation," Verbenk said from his position over her shoulder, reigning in his temper and self-loathing, "is not supposed to be performative."

"Poor baby. Failure to perform," she drawled, throwing her forearm over her eyes—and drawing the doctor's attention to a blood vessel that stood out from her temple like an angry worm. Despite her reclining position, he could see the woman was wound tight and near boiling, as she had been at the top of all their sessions so far, and by now he knew her tongue was sharp enough to draw blood when she was this worked up. "It happens to every guy now and then. Or at least, so I'm—"

"Or so you're told," he snapped, pinching the bridge of his nose, because of course she had to go there. Janet was avoidance coping, which meant deflection, deflection, deflection and bullshit—and that never-to-me nonsense was always such bullshit. "Because every woman claims to have only been *told*, don't they? So it happens to all men sometimes but no woman ever? Right."

"So you do have experience with impotence then?" Janet asked, tilting her head toward the doctor, still blindfolded by her forearm but never blind. Instead infuriatingly sighted, her telepathy having turned the bone of his skull into transparent glass. The exposure hadn't yet become easier with experience, and he doubted it ever would.

"You already know the answer to that question," said Verbenk, because there was no point in denying anything in her presence. Memories and images had already flashed across his mind of the handful of times he had experienced impotence in the sexual arena. Before she could ask more, he resigned himself to the inevitable and served up the further details on a mental silver tray.

Yes, he'd prescribed himself Viagra once, more for fun than out of real, medical need, but there. Did that make her happy?

The admission earned Verbenk a peek of her eye toward him—bloodshot beneath its mascara—as she asked, "How'd that work out for you?" A dentist's question, posed while simultaneously drilling into his head.

The doctor shifted butt cheek to butt cheek, remembering. "Not as uncomfortable as this has been."

"Gee," she said, replacing the arm blindfold in a pearl-clutching manner far too delicate for such a viper. "Thanks. Way to make my problem so thoroughly about you and all."

The doctor whined, "That's not fair."

After all, he wasn't the one making their conversations all about him. Sessions with Janet were like conducting therapy with a one-way mirror: She could read him like a book, while he knocked on glass. She was operating on a higher plane, and all his learning and experience and professionalism was suddenly juvenile and useless. He was a zoo chimp, using primitive tools to fish for ants, while she watched in a white scientist coat, scoffing at the paltry effort.

Still reclining, Janet said, "Hey, I don't want to be up there—" She wiggled her fingers over her shoulder in the

general direction of Verbenk's head, the nails bitten ragged. "— any more than you want me to be. Let's not com-
pare fairness, doc. Now try again."

"Maybe be nice to people you're asking to do things
for you?" he suggested, pressing the heels of his palms
against his eyes.

"Maybe be present for the people you're trying to help?"
she lobbed back. "The shit in your head seems a permanent situation, but my needs are a little more unique. And
pressing. Perhaps the patient should come first."

Verbenk popped another painkiller in his mouth and
awkwardly nodded as he washed it down with water. She
was perhaps mean, but also right. A puzzle was not solved
by the solver reflecting. And oh, how he longed to understand this woman, this strawberry-haired frustration clad
expensive activewear.

"First things first," he said, shoring up his mental defenses and smoothing his face into its professional mask.
"I can do first things first. In fact, with all the insistence
about meditation these first few sessions, I'm still of the
opinion that we need to fully engage with the foundation
of the psychiatric process. For instance, the onset of your
telepathy. You're certain that you weren't ill in the days
or weeks before your ability began? You weren't injured,
perhaps hit your head and wrote it off as nothing?"

Raising her wrist to show him the plasticky fitness
bracelet around it, she said, "I track my health reli-
giously. I also keep a detailed schedule of my activities."
Apparently her household lived and died by this packed,

hurry-making schedule, which often caused her phone to ding into their sessions. "I've looked at both, and I had a doctor's appointment the very day before where they ran quite a few tests. I've been tested for everything over the last year, believe me. Clean bill of health, excepting some..."

Pushing herself up to sitting, Janet looked him up and down, measuring him—and he suspected finding him lacking.

"Just some female issues you need not know and wouldn't appreciate, but what are you thinking with that question?" Janet snorted. "That you'll hit me on the head again, maybe with a frying pan, and it will all go away? I may be a caricature, but I assure you, I'm not actually a cartoon."

Intrigued, "What do you mean by that?" asked Vebenk, reaching to the side table for the patient notebook—still shockingly blank—and opening its cover. Hopefully, slowly, like a wildlife photographer reaching for the camera.

But, "'What do you mean by that?'" parroted Janet, her lips curling in derision and her tone cracking the whip. "Right. Next let's do the 'tell me about your mother' bit, shall we? I'm looking for solutions, not shrink talk."

She waved away his notebook and pen, reached for her to-go cup and drank, the coffee following all the swallowed words he couldn't pry from the woman. Finished, she pressed her lips together, sealing them shut against him.

Yes, he'd once enjoyed this work. The joy had to be around here somewhere.

Verbenk opened his mouth with his next (perfectly logical and practical) suggestion to search out medical causes for her sudden telepathy and extreme, literal empathy, but before the words could be formed, her eyes flew open and she answered, "And no neurologist consults. No MRIs."

"Even to rule out possible traumatic brain injury?" he asked in exasperation. "Which it is possible could have no other telling symptoms."

She shook her head, her hair slightly staticky from the pillow. "No other doctors. No records. We've been over this. The press are always poking around for skeletons to air. If a doctor finds something in my head, it will be news. And if they *don't* find something in my head..." In the air in front of her, she spread her hands like a headline. "'Senator's wife mentally ill.' I have not worked this hard—" She slammed a fist into the couch cushion at her hip. "—and come this far—" Another fabric-cushioned punch. "—just to be sidelined by..."

"By...?" he prompted, poising his pen above the page.

Janet prevaricated, pressing her lips together in various contortions. "I don't like surprises, is all. I like control. I like plans," she said, karate-chopping one hand into the other. Then she laid her head back on the top of the couch and looked at the ceiling. "None of this is part of the plan."

Plans. Yes. He understood that. "So help me out, then. A plan is exactly what I'm looking to create with these, to your mind silly, but to me vital questions about your health and your thoughts," said Verbenk. "We call it a treatment plan."

"A treatment plan?" Janet mocked the words, arcing her brows at him. "You want to form a treatment plan. To cure telepathy. How grandiloquent of you."

"Gah." *Women*. Men were never this tricksy. "I said—" Or thought, for that matter. "—nothing of curing. However, coping is often the next best thing to curing, and how are you coping, Janet?"

"Fine," she snapped.

He scanned her critically with his gaze. One of the few diagnostics he'd been able to use—because she couldn't stop him—was chronicling the physical effects of the telepathy: headache, spotty vision, nausea, loss of balance, speechlessness. Fainting, she'd said, though he hadn't witnessed it firsthand. There were less medical markers, as well. The bitten nails and irritability. Nervous exhaustion, he bet. Her skin was sallow at the cheeks and shiny at the forehead underneath her make-up.

Cracks in her public face—which perhaps meant cracks in her defenses today, he thought with hope. This session, she was wearing black tights that stretched up into the skirt of a sporty cotton dress. A jogger's legs, strong, and—

Dammit. Verbenk had been momentarily proud of himself. Ten minutes into the session and he hadn't thought about her body once, but a runner's ass was one of the best kinds. Before he could censor his thoughts, there was his imagined image of hers rising unbidden in his head, the talent his gift and his curse.

"Uck," she said, pulling the word up her throat. Janet raised her eyes to the heavens and rearranged the thin, voluminous scarf around her neck a little lower over her bosom and asked, "Why are you torturing me?"

Verbenk winced. The last few days, the doctor had been practicing consciously controlling his thoughts, including sessions of eyes-glazed staring at the shower wall thinking only *tile*, *tile*, *tile*, *tile* until the bathroom was filled with billowing steam. Right now, he practiced the same mindlessness, letting the steam wipe his mind clean of pretty, naked flesh so he could focus on his work. The work that was supposedly the purpose of his life, the life he'd so far fucked up so badly.

Janet took a long pull on her coffee—or rather, coffee drink, because he could smell the sugar syrup from here—and said, "And fucked it up awful good."

The sting was 10 times more powerful aloud from her lips than said privately in his head, the thought given weight through words, and there he was again under the searing light of that interrogation room, hotter and hotter. But he went back to the shower, washing clean the surface of his mind, hopefully making his deeper thoughts more slippery.

"And we're back talking about me again," he said. "For your apparently least favorite person—"

"Oh, it's a toss-up on that lately," she grumbled, setting down the cup in order to cross her arms.

"—I sure am your favorite subject of conversation." He leaned back, tented his fingers and tried to flip the tables, staring at Janet. Thinking only of the image of Janet in front of him. See how she liked the reflection treatment.

"If I'm so awfully awful, what would it hurt to talk about you for while?"

Thrusting out her jaw, "What do you know about how much it would *hurt*?" demanded Janet, but he didn't give her the victory of a response, instead pointedly holding his pen above his notebook, waiting for the words. Acting as if he had all day. Staring.

Uncomfortably working her mouth, Janet finally said, "You have no idea what I'm going through."

"Exactly." Verbenk tapped his nose, smug. "I can only know what you tell me."

She rolled her eyes, but was also tilting her head as if angling an antenna, perhaps trying to read him. Verbenk turned up the smug, making his brain foggy with smug and steam, because she couldn't criticize what she didn't see.

After several tense moments, her shoulders rose and fell with a huff. She picked at a ball of pilling on her skirt. She sucked her tongue against her teeth.

Still he waited, stretching the silence, because he seriously *did* have all day! *What should I do with all that time later?* he asked himself, although for her benefit. Maybe go online and donate money to a conservative political cause, perhaps an organization Tea Party in flavor, or he could—

"Stop." Janet broke first, saying, "You know, I fail to see why I should converse with you at all if I don't have to. I mean, come on. You had sex with a patient! Among other despicable things." She began to count on her fingers. "You're also sexist. You're sexually obsessed. You're selfish and you're dishonest and, oh god, the *angst*. Angst is the worst. Like physical pain."

Her eyes narrowed, looking for a reaction from him, tuning in, but *tile, tile, tile*, thought the doctor, who would not be baited back into vulnerability.

"Hrm," she hummed. "Also, your shoulder blade is itchy, your right knee you banged last night is beginning to ache again, and you..." She searched his face. "...you just remembered you didn't leave out a check for the cleaning lady, who's a loud-talking woman named Aneta whose hips make you think she's had many children."

Wide-eyed, Verbenk blinked, surprised not by her accuracy—he knew enough to fear her precision by now—but with the physicality and depth of these bull's-eye hits. He *had* hit his knee yesterday, against a cabinet door. Today, he'd registered the residual ache only briefly, when he'd shifted and crossed his legs. And yes, Aneta's always-scolding tone rather scared him. She wore a tiny cross around her neck and he imagined she had a direct line to a vengeful Catholic God that could smite Verbenk down in his own home, but that thought had been buried deep beneath other more active thought processes.

"You get all of that from me?" he asked in amazement. "Those thoughts—and sensations even—are far from top of mind."

Rubbing at her temple, "All that and more. Just layers and layers of information." Her words were breathy and exhausted. "Reading minds, it's not a narrative like in a book like you might expect, but more of a tidal wave of the people around me. In this case, a tidal wave of *you*. I swear, if not for your location..."

Pushing a word in edgewise, "Meaning I'm a neighbor?" he asked.

"Sure, but you're off the beaten path here," said Janet, holding out her arms in a protective bubble as example. "The cul-de-sac, the open space behind, this big yard in front—" He reflexively turned to look out the window behind him, which framed the side courtyard and its rose bushes. (*Fuck.* The gardener needed paying, too.) "There aren't cars or passers-by or noise. I can see why you like hiding here."

Interesting. Proximity, he realized, was a component of her ability. Janet had a range. Of course Janet had a range, he now thought, but that fact had been too obvious to be pertinent before, during the forced marches to the beach that made up the whole of their first three appointments.

Still, such facts put concrete edges on her magical ability, and the realities of telepathy versus his comic-book assumptions were fascinating. The telepathic Supers he remembered were all action: creating mind rays to control the masses, communicating across vast distances, usually a good dose of telekinesis thrown in for good measure. They were not targets; they were not afflicted. But here Janet was receiving layers of sensory information passively, against her will. She was being acted upon by the ability.

Tentative excitement, like the first bubbles of heating water, tickled Verbenk, who asked, "So being around people, probably and especially larger groups of people, must be your biggest challenge, yes? Can you give me an example?"

"Easily." Apparently too worked up to care she'd started cooperating, "Which horror do you want first?" asked Janet, gesturing melodramatically. "Let's go over what's happened to me in just the last twenty-four hours. For example, the florist for tonight's event. Have you ever felt the itch of serious psoriasis?" Her lip curled in distaste. "Oh, and in writing him a check, now I know that he's operating under a fake name because he's wanted for child support in Arizona."

Verbenk cringed, especially disgusted at the overheard sensory information. Experiencing how it felt inside someone else's skin—just any random stranger's—sounded disgusting. Like licking the bathroom door handle on an airplane.

"Apt metaphor, but then get this," Janet continued, the words beginning to flow now after being pent up without company for so long. "I went to the grocery store this morning, and the forty-seven-year-old woman who checked my groceries? She's giving the bag boy hand jobs in exchange for part of his government-assistant check. I mean, he's eighteen—barely—but also developmentally disabled, and Jesus fucking Christ, what is wrong with people?"

This time he recoiled outright, shaking his head like a dog and purposefully not asking which store, which checker, because he didn't want to know.

"And I don't want to know either," she replied. "That's the problem. I'm like, 'I'm here for bananas, not your life story.' Maybe that sounds awful, but I don't want to absorb the blurry confusion of the new mother on Aisle Two. I don't need to know that your father just died with your issues unresolved when I stand in line to pick up a prescription."

"That does sound like a reasonable request," answered Verbenk. His pen was now back where it belonged: in his hand, scribbling away. He was back in his element: listening, connecting the dots. Taking advantage of the segue, he added, "And how is the prescription working? The Valium?"

Shifting on the couch, Janet pulled her skirt further down her thighs, then seemed to curl further into herself.

"It just makes it worse," she said wistfully, likely having hoped for a magic-bullet medication to make it all better. They all did. "Valium is like drowning in the tidal wave but *while drunk* instead, when I can barely keep my wits about me sober. And I cannot look like an idiot. I mean, the two times I saw myself when on the Valium, I looked a mess. My eyes were all—"

"Wait," said Verbenk, waving his hand, unable to resist the meaty aroma of the offhand comment. "Saw yourself?"

She smiled a dark little smile. "Ah," she answered in the universal tone of worm-can opening. Verbenk wrinkled his nose in delight, his instincts proven yet again. "That's some of the worst. Getting to see myself reflected in everyone else's eyes. Hardly need a mirror to get dressed in the morning, and it happens even with people who are supposed to be..." She swallowed. "Oh, never mind."

He would have sworn she was embarrassed. He had no idea why. For him, all this information was thrilling.

"There's no never-minding now, Janet," said Verbenk, who was on the edge of his seat, because this was his habitat, exploring the murky, musky depths of the human experience. He loved picking apart the tangled threads of emotion and motivation in his patients' lives, always one for puzzles, living for that satisfying click of discovery, of bringing chaos into order.

But perhaps in reaction to his growing pleasure, Janet shut back down, remembering herself. Unwilling to grant him any victory. How fucking frustrating! And just when they were getting going, which made the lack of cooperation even more maddening. Why did every relationship he had with a woman seem to turn into passive-aggressive siege warfare?

She snorted prettily. "Do you really want my opinion about your sporadic but disgustingly unhealthy relationships with women?"

"No." The doctor cleared his throat. "Um, no. But look. If you're really that dead-set on not talking to anyone else about this ability *and* you can't handle it yourself—"

She muttered, "Like you could?"

Though his jaw clenched, he continued. "—then you should consider cooperating, talking to me."

Venbenk tapped pen against page, re-reading his notes to see what had catalyzed her into speech just moments earlier. He must have done something, said something. Normally his housewives were so keen to chat that he needed only nod or insert an encouraging word now and then. Such women seemed starved for ears, into which they poured their own ideas about themselves, creating self-portraits of flattering truths.

A luxury Janet no longer had, actually.

"Quite a double blow for you," he observed, cocking his head to watch his prey. "Not feeling comfortable in crowds and also being keenly aware of how you're presenting yourself. I can't think of a more trying challenge than telepathy for someone like you, a politician's wife—"

"Oh, shut up with that shit," she said, snapping her chin at him like a boxer. "You act like women are a different species or something. Housewife this, politician's wife that. I'm more than a fucking wife. I'm a political operative."

She leaned forward until she was perched on the edge of the leather couch. "I've worked in campaigns for most of my adult life, at the local, state and national levels. I started out gathering signatures for ballot initiatives outside grocery stores next to all the Girl Scouts and their cookies. I'm a community organizer, on social media and door-to-door when I have to, and when I work the phones, a campaign gets results. I'm personally responsible for millions of dollars raised." He was lucky her pointed finger wasn't a real weapon. "Millions."

Verbenk narrowed his eyes, shaping his thoughts. So maybe he was an ass. He'd give her that. He was not above thinking the same of himself on occasion (all the time), but it seemed that when he goaded and really assholed it up, Janet talked.

"So you've raised millions for all those annoying campaign ads that clog up my TV? You are personally responsible for all those robo-calls? Oh, bravo," he said, golf-clapping around his pen. "Definitely a calling, that. And you don't even get the prize at the end: the power. How fulfilling that work must be."

Janet pursed her lips, shook her strawberry hair and looked at Verbenk as if *he* were developmentally disabled. "I see what you're doing there, doc."

The doctor shrugged. "I don't think it matters. I think most of the reason you're upset is because..." He'd red-flagged an odd phrase she'd used earlier, and now turned it around to face her. "I'm guessing that the self you see reflected in other people's eyes is not what you want to be but instead a crude *caricature* of a—" Verbenk raked her up and down with his cruelest judgement filter. "—pretty, vain white girl who married up and has never seen a day of hardship in her life."

If it had an edge, her glare could have cut off his balls—but he'd never been so thrilled at the idea of castration, because he could tell he'd hit the right button.

"Yes, yes," said Janet, whose face was red but who so far was penning her anger, even if it was straining at the fence. "You think you're so smart, don't you? Always sizing people up, making insulting guesses about their lives. Though I admit, those guesses can be uncannily accurate. Like that first day and the sorority thing."

Taken aback, "Sorority?" he replied, confused whether she was being intentionally cryptic or if being telepathic made her assume he could read her mind, as well. "Help the non-telepath here."

Janet sighed in exasperation. "That first session? You sized me up, and you guessed that I was president of my sorority, like it was written on my forehead—and like it was this horrible thing. And you were right." A dark, little laugh. "People are so skilled at making me hate things I like about myself."

Verbenk's memory was jogged. He'd been gauging her type: maybe a soloist, maybe a public speaker, maybe president of a group of perky college co-eds with more Mardi Gras beads than brains. He attempted to *tile*, *tile*, *tile* over the image of how such ladies traditionally lifted their tops to earn those beads.

Funny, though, that he'd been right.

"I'll have you know," Janet said, smoothing her hair, "that in my case, sorority life was about a lot more than partying. Being elected president of Alpha Theta Pi was how I found my calling in public service. Soon I was volunteering for local political campaigns—"

Meeting hot, older male candidates.

She stomped her foot, but did her best to otherwise ignore him, barely pausing. "—and discovered I had a knack for leadership. Politics is not some game to me. It's high-stakes work that affects the lives of millions of Americans. On good days, it's the joy of solving real problems for real people, the amazing high of getting shit done." She emphasized the last phrase with three points of her finger, confident in her skills of persuasion.

What a focus-grouped response. She'd obviously worked on some version of that life story with a PR pro, even if the cursing was her own frosting.

"Gah! How do you do that? Fine. That's true, too." She threw her hands in the air. "But forgive me if I want to have a purposeful life. I really believe people should try to give back, to be of service, maybe make the world a better place. Sue me."

Verbenk's eyebrows rose two inches. He'd finally stolen a peek under this woman's confident shell, only to find the squeaky-cleanest secret he'd ever unearthed: Janet Buckmann was an honest-to-goodness do-gooder, someone who—still, as an adult who'd long known there was no Santa Claus—believed that politics of all things was actually a vector for positive change. In fact, she believed it was somehow her Purpose, which he pictured with an uppercase P in pink ink. How cute, how very—

"I am not naive," Janet snapped.

"I was thinking more like... idealistic," Verbenk replied, unfazed, because oh, how meaty. How delicious. He juggled these tidbits and traits, forming a tentative personality profile, working out these issues like math, scribbling his initial answers.

"Tell me," said Janet sarcastically, narrowing her eyes. "Are you just out of practice, or have you never had a genuine emotional connection in your life? Are all your clients just clinical problems you enjoy solving, or am I the only lucky one?"

Hurt, the doctor's bottom lip stuck out. "Hey, I didn't mean—"

"Never mind. It doesn't matter," she said. "I guess I knew what I was up against from the start, but this stupid telepathy has shown me how fucked I am. I really can't win, can I? According to people's minds, apparently I'm both ugly and vain, too smart and secretly stupid, too fat and too thin. They think I'm an ice queen. They think I'm a slut." She smiled sarcastically. "Sometimes at the same time, just for kicks!"

And if she was as image-conscious as he suspected, even the mildest detected negativity would chafe. Repeated exposure of the type she described would cheese-grate her feelings to hamburger.

Ignoring that stray opinion, Janet streamed on, "I'm never enough. I'm *insufficient*. According to everyone and their neighbor, I'm nothing but another power-hungry, out-for-herself bitch, sleeping her way into political power."

Well... Fuck this radical transparency, because now Janet knew he'd at least partially assumed the same. Her husband's family wealth and field, the age difference: The gold- and/or power-digger archetype was an easy assumption.

"You, too?" she asked. "Figures."

He held up his hands. *Briefly*, he made sure to send, and before he actually knew her.

Janet raised her finger in objection. "These people whose thoughts I wade through, every day, all day long, none of them know me, either, and the 'bitch' part is pretty universal," she admitted—and Verbenk thought her more puzzled than upset by the thought. "So don't talk to me about what harm it could do to talk about the telepathy. It's painful. All of it. Forgive me if I don't want to relive how everyone sees me, but no one sees me, and how it doesn't matter because none of them like me anyway."

Nodding rapidly as he wrote, the doctor could empathize completely, because Janet was constantly holding up a warped reflection of himself to Verbenk. It was her favorite deflection. It wasn't fun.

"Why have I dedicated my life to helping people who hate me?" she said, letting her frustration bloom. "Why do I try to help people who lie, like, *all the fucking time?* Because all people lie. All of it, just lies and cowardice."

If his goal was to get her steaming and communicative, mission accomplished. Verbenk watched her passion with delight. This woman was genuinely interesting, her anger not of the teary or spittle-flying varieties, but instead hot and sharp. Leaning toward the coffee table, she tried to drink from her cup only to find it empty. She held it vertically upside down above her mouth, even shook it, then grrr-ed in anger directly at the innocent green logo, as if the poor mermaid was to blame.

How obsessed she'd been with the damn cup all day, holding it as if it were both life jacket and bulletproof vest. In fact, he realized, excepting that first meeting, he'd never seen Janet without a hot beverage in her hand. *Hmmmm*. Something was going on with that coffee, and his instinctual guesses had been right on lately, so he said, "The coffee hasn't lied to you, Janet."

"No," she said. "It just judges me, too."

He leaned back and tented his fingers in excitement and pride. He was enjoying this whole goading-her-into-cooperation scheme, in part because the more he thought about the technique, the angrier—and more forthcoming—she became. "What's with the coffee, Janet?"

Slumping, "Please don't make me go there," she said—an admission by omission. Janet went in for another sip, but paused with the traitorous empty cup halfway to her mouth and emitted a frightening, feminine growl before practically tossing it onto the end table nearest the doctor. The doctor saw only now that it was labeled in black with her misspelled name: Janette. "I don't want to talk about it."

"Too bad," he said. Verbenk was tangled now, deep in the puzzle, and he wanted to know. *Needed* to know.

He felt immersed in her story, engaged in a way he hadn't been in a long time. Can't-put-it-down interested. Flashlight-reading-after-bedtime interested, much like when he was a little boy with his *Superman* and *Strange Tales* and *The Fantastic Four* and *X-Men*, stories of much more consequence than his insignificant little life because those heroes had power. They could save people when young Verbenk couldn't save anyone, everything and everyone careening toward disaster in those days despite his best efforts.

Now this woman sat before Verbenk with real superpowers, in the midst of a real-life superhero crisis, but she didn't want to talk about it? Unacceptable.

"Well, you can't make me," pouted Janet, unnerved into petulance.

Verbenk licked his lips, ready for the challenge. "Oh? How about you tell me about the coffee, whatever that happens to mean to you and/or your telepathy," he warned, "or I could think more about myself. Such as..." He cast around the room, and the laptop on his desk gave him an idea. He began to mentally catalog his favorite adult websites, those he had bookmarked under the innocuously titled category: research.

"Please! Don't," begged Janet, showing him her palms in surrender. "Fine. I just... I don't want to. It's personal."

"This is therapy," he said. "That's part and parcel, and look, we all have unflattering secrets. I'll put aside the commentary, OK? I promise I'll listen and not judge, whatever this caffeinated secret is." Or at least, he telepathically promised, he'd really, really try.

Staring, reading him, she seemed to gauge his honesty. Verbenk bit his lip and mentally crossed his fingers. Therapy was a dance, and like a dance, it was easy to step on toes. But when you got the timing and personal chemistry just right, the interplay could be viscerally thrilling—but only, you know, when dealing with *other* people's problems. One's own were so much more sensitive. To prove his worth, he *tile, tile, tiled* over his internal monologue to the best of his abilities, making himself into a receptive sauna of listening.

"All right, all right. The coffee thing, then." Janet smoothed her hair, then placed one hand atop the other on her lap. After a dramatic pause, she said with gravitas, "It's Orin. My husband."

The pen hung, waiting. Waiting in vain as the moment of silence stretched. "What about Orin?" he asked.

For the first time in their short acquaintance, Janet's eyes filled with tears. "Hold on," she said, blinking her masacara-ed lashes rapidly. "I'm getting there. It's... emotional."

"Take your time."

Sniff. "It was...," Janet began tentatively. "It was the very first morning of the telepathy, actually. The big kick-off of this totally non-super ability." Another sniff, another stall. "I walked into the kitchen, and Greg had been there already. That's Orin's chief of staff. He's often downstairs at work in Orin's home office before we are, and he'd left me coffee. Venti raspberry white-chocolate mocha. Skinny, double shot."

Venti berry choco-whu? He couldn't help it. Verbenk's mind betrayed his common sense and scoffed. Something as ridiculous and foofy as that uber-specific sugary coffee cocktail couldn't possibly be as emotionally charged as

Janet was leading on. This was drive-thru material. This was as housewifey as a housewife could get.

Though these thoughts skittered through his head for only a split second, Janet's eyebrows fell instantly into a scowl and she clanged shut against him.

Verbenk cursed his negativity reflex which, like his hindsight, had betrayed him. Fantasy and silent word play had always amused him, but Janet had sucked all the fun right out of both. Genuinely, he said, "I'm sorry." He set aside his notebook, disarming himself, and held out his palms. "Really. I'm sorry. Please, go on. You came down to the kitchen. Then what?"

Another sniff was his only answer. He imagined himself as a giant ear with no other purpose but to hear this woman, and he saw her jaw unclench a few degrees. Then her shoulders drooped too far to be a sign of mere apology acceptance. A much heavier burden than he'd expected was contained within her empty to-go cup.

"Please," repeated Verbenk. "Go on."

"I suppose you're actually illustrating my point." She briefly closed her eyes, holding out her hand as if the kitchen that morning was replicated in her palm. "OK. So I'm reaching for my coffee, and Orin comes up behind me."

Verbenk could see them now, the perfect picture. Orin would probably stride into the kitchen wearing a Capitol-quality suit and one of surely many ties of patriotic blue, not a hair out of place. (None of it balding either, damn the man. Verbenk was only 10 or so years older.) Handsome, rich, high-society family, charming. What woman could resist him?

"Normally, not me," quipped Janet. "Normally he comes up behind me, kisses my neck, wishes me good morning and then goes about making his own coffee. He's a bit of a snob, you see, has this whole process for it. Burr grinder, Guatemalan beans, cold-brew pour-over artisan whatever-it-is made in Italy. But instead of good morning, this time I hear, 'First ladies *don't* drink mochas. Her immaturity is showing again. ' Clear as a bell."

The doctor blinked. "Come again?"

Janet pulled the most violent—and frankly, impressive—eye roll he'd ever seen in his life. "His political ambitions, idiot. *Our* political ambitions. It's no secret between us that he has eyes on the governor's mansion." To Verbenk's surprise, her voice broke with hurt despite her anger, the two emotions entwined as she continued, "It's not like Orin and I haven't been open about what we want from the start, OK? You have to be. We're nothing if not practical people."

Well, perhaps ambitious first.

"That, too," she admitted. "But I thought we were on the same page, on the same team, and he doesn't think I'm first lady material? I don't measure up, and it worries him, more than I ever would have guessed."

"You don't measure up, because of your coffee order?"

Janet pushed away the box of tissues he proffered as if he was offering offense, insisting on wiping her eyes with the back of her wrists. "Apparently my mochas make me look young, frivolous and unserious. I always knew that politics is about image, but I had no fucking idea how far it went. The math going on in that man's head about me, weighing me, judging me for an audience. It was... illuminating. And hurtful."

Understanding washed over Verbenk's features. Latte as a symbol wielded by someone who was supposed to love unconditionally. While the doctor genuinely felt her hurt feelings—tender and eggplant-colored, aching—this sympathy existed side by side with a sense of peace. He leaned back, seeing the shape of it now, like a lens focusing, the first sense emerging from blur.

Janet seemed in control again. Her color fading, exposing the subtle freckles on her cheekbones, she said, "Because that's the number one stereotype I embody, right? The younger woman. For him to be taken seriously, *I* need to be taken seriously. He wants to avoid looking like a trophy-wife hunter, or worse, a cradle robber. Even though, I mean, he's only twelve years older."

Only? *Tile, tile, tile.* Verbenk swallowed all his reflexes and listened.

"I admit. I always liked his maturity," she said, a flicker of a smile crossing her lips. "Boys don't become men until they age a bit, you know? And he could introduce me to the finer things in life, guide me, when boys my age were still all about beer bongs."

A smile also quirked Verbenk's lips. The sophisticated older man, introducing the then even-younger Janet to life's pleasures. Wine and expensive dinners. Sex on high-thread-count sheets. Verbenk had also always loved the way he looked in a younger woman's eyes—

Stop it. This was not about him.

Janet nodded approval at his correction. "You're right, though," she said with a shrug. "But now I know the truth of it, all from his own head. How it really needles him about the mochas. How it was not really my idea to get my teeth whitened last year. It was his. The wine I buy—not beer—how I dress—Marc Jacobs, mostly, when on camera—our political platform. Even my friends, to a certain extent. He's subtly chosen them all for me. The man has a focus group in his damn head, and it's brutal. And that, doc, is the coffee thing."

Her expressive hands dropped at that point and she turned to gauge his expression, as if she was issuing him a challenge: Let's see what you do with that.

What *was* he going to do with that?

The doctor shifted in his chair, his mind blank. He may have been over-confident. Now that she was playing therapy ball, he felt maybe he wasn't at the top of his game, and it was dawning on him that he'd been off that game for a long time. He hadn't been this challenged or had to think this deeply about a patient's problems for years.

"That must have felt very..." Not having personal experience that seemed relevant, he was forced to dig deeper and place himself into her sporty little shoes. "Jarring. Belittling," he finally settled on, and Janet nodded enthusiastically, for once seeming to be interested in what he had to say.

"But," he continued, splicing together his thoughts, "so much of that is just ego, isn't it? I guess the important thing is: Does he love you, under all that crap? You'd know for sure now, right?"

Softening, "Yeah," she said, and the admission seemed to give her comfort. "Yeah, he loves me, and poor guy, he *does* have the wits to keep those things to himself. It's not his fault his wife has eavesdropping superpowers." The corners of her lips turned up. "I think the actual thought phrasing was: 'First Ladies don't make the motorcade stop for lattes.'" She snorted.

Oh, he had a motorcade in this fantasy, too. How important.

Janet didn't want to tease her husband, though. "He also genuinely cares about his job. A lot. It's exhausting following it all, honestly, racing around his head. It's nice they're in session and he's not always home."

She subsided into contemplation, and the fascinated doctor felt cheated she wasn't inviting him along. He waited several moments for more, still stuck in that kitchen—the blue tie, the dueling coffees, the unanswered subtext—puzzling and attempting to sharpen that focus.

"So....?" he finally led, repressing the urge to bounce in his seat like a little boy left waiting by a "To Be Continued" non-conclusion. Janet could already hear his unanswered questions, of course. She didn't have to make him ask aloud, but he did nonetheless, saying, "So what did you do? I mean, you're standing there in the kitchen and you hear your first thought—*that* first thought—and what did you do?"

A wicked-edged smile cracked her face. "Well, something that ridiculous bothering him? Like my mocha defines me? Fuck that. I went to Starbucks twice that day, and I've done the same every day since, just to peeve him," she said, thrusting out her chin. "Tell me who to be, will you? Nope."

A huge pig-snort of a laugh erupted from Verbenk's nostrils, dramatic enough that he was forced to cough several times, knocking a fist on his chest.

Janet's nose wrinkled in shared mirth. "I know, right? It's driving him crazy, though he hasn't dared to say anything out loud."

Over on the desk, his phone buzzed. The signal for the end of their session. Verbenk double checked his watch, but sure enough. Once she'd gotten rolling, the rest of their session had passed in a flash, and they'd reached such a wonderful, thought-provoking stopping place. The first planks in the bridge of trust had been built, and self-congratulation was definitely in order. He didn't suck as bad today as most days!

"What?" Janet asked, frantically looking from him to his phone and back. "No. We don't need to stop right this moment, do we? You don't have any other clients today. Your only other appointment is with a bottle of wine."

Or maybe a Grey Goose martini tonight, Verbenk thought, glowing with pleasure. Martinis made hard liquor civilized, and he was feeling fucking civilized. Alexander the Fucking Great, breaking down city walls, bringing Roman order to the recalcitrant masses. This fencing match of a conversation was perhaps the breakthrough-est session he'd led in a long time. He stood, stretching his arms. He'd done something good today, so maybe after she'd absented herself, a nap was—

But Janet dribbled her feet like a basketball in (childish) objection, knees bouncing.

"But after I told you all that, spilled my guts, we haven't gone to the beeeeeaaaach," she whined. "I don't want promising therapeutic process. I want relief! Please? Please. You're feeling better, and I have this black-tie gala tonight. The first one I've personally organized. It's a big deal. I need to be at my best!" She supplicated with puppy eyes.

Right. She had mentioned some shindig tonight, hadn't she? Something about a florist, so he pictured an event with powerful people laughing with crystal wine glasses and very white teeth and four-figure donations per plate funneled into funds to be used for more of those annoying TV ads.

Shaking her head in adorable earnestness, Janet said, "It's not a campaign event. This is *my* project. A fundraiser for Love International, an aid organization for child refugees from around the world. And I've been cooperative, haven't I? It's a cause that means the world to me."

Emotions roiled across her face, emotions Verbenk couldn't place. She was literally pleading now, her hands pressed together, as children were taught to pray.

"There will be two hundred people there, likely with horrible secrets and wild emotions, and I can't fuck this up," she whispered. "I can't. It's important."

His self-satisfaction disappeared under the idea of tidal waves and pummeling layers of information. Of the energy it must take to hold the ego whole under the face of constant, unfiltered criticism. Quite a tailor-made challenge the universe had crafted for Janet, and he noticed again her poor nails, uneven and red, exposed.

Quickly hiding those fingers under her thighs, she went on, "If we could just meditate, just for a few minutes, just to reset me back to zero, then I think I can handle it. I'll get through."

The poor woman. Inhaling his resignation at the nap delay, he settled himself more comfortably in the chair as if settling into a throne.

Within milliseconds of his decision to relent, Janet was on her back, head upon pillow, her forearm swooned over her eyes. "Thank you. Thankyouthankyouthankyou. You're saving my life."

The corner of Verbenk's mouth cracked a smile, and perhaps the edifice of his self-loathing cracked a bit, too, because look at that: He was needed. Still, not one to be ordered around, he decided he was tired of the water. With florists so recently on his mind, he was drawn instead to look out his office window.

Roses, glorious in the afternoon sun. Beautiful. Delicate but strong. He closed his eyes and concentrated on the roses, meditated on the messy simplicity of flowers, which were both regular and predictable, but each one unique. Their breath—his and Janet's—was the stir of breeze through the petals. Together they felt the nurturing heat of the sun, the stability of earth-gripping roots, reaching and growing.

Funny. He hadn't given a woman roses in years.

"Verbenk…" Janet warned from the couch, and embarrassed, he slammed down the wall to his inner life and made it climb with roses.

3

"**N**o," Verbenk said into the patient intercom at the ungodly hour of 6:45 a.m. the next morning. His tongue was still sleep-fuzzy, and he swallowed, needing water—needing to go back to bed—before adding for good measure, "No way. Uh-uh. Go home. It's too early."

"It is not that early," said Janet's transmitted voice through the wall-mounted speaker near the door. Not having stopped for his glasses in his startlement, she appeared only a fleshy, fish-eyed blob through the peephole. He should have locked the outer gate.

"You aren't bleeding, far as I can see," he noted, "so go away."

"I'll explain," Janet said, striving for a tone of cheerful normality. "Let me in."

But Verbenk shook his head. No. He could give her an appointment at eleven o'clock if she was willing, and surely whatever it was could wait four hours. A man needed some warning. Verbenk needed that much respect at least. He also needed to pee—and was uncomfortable with Janet knowing he needed to pee. He was uncomfortable with Janet seeing the out-of-fashion chest hair poofing from the low V of his robe. He pulled the two sides together tighter and retied the robe's belt.

The intercom transmitted a resigned sigh. "I suppose I can allow you to dress. Can I just wait in your—"

"No," he said, cutting her off with a press of the interior talk button, remembering that Janet had a range. If he let her in, he could just imagine: Janet sitting primly on the couch down in his office, perhaps wincing as she "overheard" the sensation of Verbenk in another part of the house putting on his pants, leg hair against cotton. Janet even feeling for herself the relief of that pent-up morning whizz.

"Come on. Your office is so isolated and calm," said Janet.

But he merely repeated, "Too early," while stifling a yawn, still feeling in the grips of sleep, which he'd only found a few hours ago.

High on breakthrough, he'd spent much of the night in the badly lit basement with an ancient, D-battery-thick flashlight—and a half bottle of vodka—searching for his childhood boxes. His comics. After all, Sherman had never said he'd destroyed his nephew's belongings; it was much more like his uncle to shove away and repress the distasteful.

Sure enough, the now-old Verbenk had finally located the young man's treasures in the form of two corner-smashed boxes. Smaller than he remembered, each fit easily under one arm, and inside he'd found plastic toy soldiers, playing cards, two left-hand woolen mittens, a Boy Scout guide to birds, and a handful of the pulpy, powerful paper books he'd come searching for.

Archie. Casper. Superman: "The UNDERSEA PRANKS of MR. MXYZPTLK!" With the yellowed book on his knees, he'd read into the wee hours of Mxyzptlk's ridiculous manipulations of Superman, basically a Rumpelstiltskin tale in spandex involving an undersea battle and a submarine turned into a banana. Then the X-Men. Four clean-cut teenagers being put through their paces by Professor X—a powerful telepath himself—honing their powers in crazy, obstacle-course-like training exercises.

With his mind still full of spandex and bananas, he'd never be able to replicate yesterday's success.

"I have certain professional standards," he told Janet, "and I think you'd want me to treat you like any other patient who—"

"Remember Sandra?" asked Janet, and he could hear the words were delivered through clenched teeth. "I can still talk, you know. Let me in."

He punched the button with his thumb again, hissing, "It's also early for blackmail, too."

After a momentary pause, "Please," she said softly into the intercom, obviously bringing her mouth close. He pictured her looking vulnerably behind her toward the street, as if for prying eyes. "I have nowhere else to go."

His eyes fell shut. Did they teach all women to play the heartstrings, just as in upper-crust homes such as this one, they'd once taught prim little girls the piano and embroidery and French. (*Mal*. Bad man. Bad, bad man.)

Muttering, Verbenk tried to rub the furrows out of his forehead, reminding himself that he'd begged for a challenging case. Here she was at his door, pain in the ass that she was, and the woman who'd been so stubbornly closed-mouthed with him just yesterday, had—heartstring flourish—nowhere else to go.

Of course he was going to let her in, if only she'd give him—

"Twenty minutes is fine," she said quickly, as if he might change his mind. "I'll be back." She released the button, but then just as Verbenk turned to trudge away, yawning, she cut back in over the speaker, asking, "Wait, do you get the newspaper?"

"What?" he asked the empty air of the book-shelved room.

The intercom: "No? OK, then."

He went back to the door, leaned into the peephole to make sure she was gone—he saw the gate clicking shut— then scratched his ass and went to shower, shaking his head in confusion.

Twenty minutes later, still tired, Verbenk was sliding into his chair, tucking a stray shirttail into his pants behind the shelter of his imposing desk—on top of which

Janet slapped down the slim local section of the morning's *Denver Post*, before striding over the couch with purpose.

"I don't know why I bother," she said, trailing the smell of her Starbucks, the acquisition of which likely filled up her time while he hurriedly showered and shaved and wondered and suspected.

"Accurate again, asshole," answered Janet. Stripping off a black fitness jacket, she had on bright running sneakers, short running shorts, and a tank top with a T-strapped back that showed off the definition of the (young) muscles in her back and shoulders. He didn't catch himself until she coughed, then asked, "Do I need to keep the jacket on?"

He tilted his head in capitulation. Right. Fantasies no longer hurt no one.

Despite her obvious fitness, she then collapsed onto his couch as if boneless. "Everyone's an asshole. All of them."

Trying to gather his wits, "The event last night?" he asked nervously. "Did it not go well?"

"No comment." Janet popped the top off an orange prescription bottle. "Xanax," she said, answering his unverbalized question. "Got it from a friend, as most people do."

When Verbenk moved to recommend against, her glare made him retreat in self-preservation.

"Shhhh." She washed down a pill with her drink, which she then set on the coffee table and leaned her head back into the cushions, eyes closed but face pained. "Just let me sit for a moment here in peace. Read," she commanded, waving a floppy hand in the direction of the paper.

And so Verbenk flipped through the newspaper pages, scanning. After a minute, he landed on what must have been the page in question, the article in question. If it could even be called an article. Blurb was more like. The headline read, "Human Rights Commissioner calls refugee situation 'dire.'" Below the headline, a man in glasses and a groomed goatee stood on stage with a mic pinned to his lapel, a 6-foot slideshow photo behind him of a family of three: bearded dad, veiled mom and a somber-eyed elementary-aged girl.

The caption read, *UN Human Rights Commission deputy director Fares Al-Kilani speaks at a benefit for Love International at the Ellie Caulkins Opera House.*

Verbenk skimmed the few paragraphs covering the event, looking for Janet's name, looking for some horrible embarrassment or offense or scene caused by her secret superability to provoke something like this surprise visit. A fist fight, a medical emergency, but there was nothing of the sort. Only a quote from Al Kilani's remarks, some statistics, then an amount raised, about $125,000. Only the bland usual, and only one other quote, from her husband.

"The plight of refugees worldwide is a complex and pressing issue, one currently without clear-cut solutions," said Sen. Orin Buckmann, in attendance with wife Janet Buckmann, who chairs the local Love International effort. "We should do all we can to draw attention to the plight of these innocent families and children. All they want is the American dream."

And that was it.

Verbenk was confused. "So why am I not still snoring?" he asked, refolding the broadsheet pages and taking off his old-man reading glasses, reaching for her patient notebook.

Opening her eyes, rubbing her temple, Janet said, "Well, it's a disaster, isn't it?"

Still not understanding, he bit first his top lip then his bottom one. "What part of it?"

"The part where I tossed months of my life and slices of my sanity down the toilet. That's what." Still looking pained, she took several more swallows of her coffee. "The part where I don't even know why I try."

Furrowing his eyebrows sadly did nothing to further his understanding. "So... which part of it?" he repeated.

She huffed, "I should have known you wouldn't understand," and then she descended back into stony silence.

"Janet?" prodded Verbenk, but still she sat, staring into the corner of his office vaguely. Just a statue, as animate as those in the garden outside. Which he found frustrating, to say the least, after her emotional plea to be let in. Here he was again, knocking on glass. Glass he'd thought they'd broken through only yesterday.

And so the doctor set his jaw, perhaps finally fully awake. The morning had been too hasty for a tie, so for a gesture of authority, he settled for adjusting his collar— and his fingertip brushed bristle, a patch of neck hastily shaven. His lack of appearance-cultivation disturbed him, made him feel wrong-footed, but he attempted nonetheless to don his armor of steam and professionalism.

"Janet, you came to me this morning," said Verbenk. "You must have done so for some articulable reason. Now what's wrong?"

With a snap, she came back to life, springing to her feet and over to his desk to poke two fingers atop the article, with so much force you'd think she wanted to hurt the newsprint.

"This is wrong." Eyes wide and fiery, she laughed darkly and began to pace the floor in front of his desk in athletic strides, gesticulating broadly. Verbenk watched her to-go cup, as if his careful eyes alone could keep the liquid inside instead of the mocha-berry-whatever splashing onto his expensive Persian rug.

"The better question," she streamed on, gale-force in her anger, ignoring his internal monolog, "is what the fuck is wrong with people. Huh?" Now she violently poked the air in front of the doctor, making him feel responsible for all people, making him pull back. She continued pacing.

"Maybe I'm here because you're the worst person I know," said Janet. "So maybe you have the answer, right? To the question what's wrong with people? I mean, when saving lives is—" She waggled her shoulders and air quoted, her lip curled in distaste. "—not 'politically expedient.' Or rather, when it's 'not the right political climate' to give a shit. That was the phrase in all their minds, behind all their smiles last night."

The doctor flicked back to the article, startled. Her complaint was not at all what he'd expected. Her husband receiving more spotlight than she had, her hard work going unnoticed: that complaint seemed in character. But those spotlighted words were still all positive.

Janet, however, had worked herself up into a rage.

"Oh, it's all perfect on the surface. I made sure of that, I made that illusion possible, but you weren't there. No one was there the way I was, of course, but let me tell you, no one was as kumbaya as that article leads on. It wasn't all about human decency and the brotherhood of man." She slurped her drink, striding, legs like scissor blades, wounding the air. "A bad political climate. As if it's climate change we're talking about—which should *not* be a subject for debate, either, but that's just one more way humans in general are pretty much the worst. The worst!"

Her passion and her frantic movement were making Verbenk's already sensitive stomach turn, having had no breakfast. His alcohol-tender eyes strained to follow, and still watching the cup, he said, "Janet, could you—?"

"'Good effort, bad timing.' That's what the article doesn't quote people as saying, but I know. I heard. Oh, what's that?" Janet gestured, as if to an invisible companion. "Their suffering could have been better timed, Senator Villabrand? So sorry the Syrian civil war is coinciding with a rise of populist xenophobia in your backwater district, but—"

"Sit down!" Verbenk finally commanded, half-lifting his tired ass from his chair and channeling the demeanor of the intimidating nuns of his Catholic schooling. Despite the dissipation of the intervening years, he found the imitation still effective.

Or at least, Janet allowed herself to appear chastened. She placed her cup primly down on the coffee table, making a point of grabbing a coaster while she pinned him with her eyes. Then she sat down with a grunt, her arms locked shut, a ball of aggression pulled into itself.

The doctor pressed his forehead with his thumbs, shoving the scrambled brains back inside. "That's better," he said. "And now in a significantly lower volume, you were saying about Senator Vil—"

"Oh, you should have seen the math in that man's head—though I should explain," said Janet. "There's rumor of a refugee bill coming up in the Senate, and Villabrand was considering supporting it. Then he literally calculated possible lost lives versus possible lost votes—honest, with pen and paper—and guess which came out more important? And his mother was an immigrant, can you imagine? Asshole!"

"Right, right, we're all assholes," said Verbenk, rolling his hands to lead her toward the real point. "This can't be news."

A quick, dark laugh. Janet bent down to scratch her exposed calf, and Verbenk couldn't help picturing that calf encased in stockings, the foot capped in a designer heel, the dress she must have worn for the occasion sparkly. Then he saw in his mind all the other important people in their finery in the lobby of the Opera House. A flock of black formalwear. No, weren't a group of black birds called a murder? A murder of other rich, dilettante housewives and politicos as well as CEOs and pundits and philanthropists. Gilded lobby, gilded people.

"And silver tongues, the politicians especially," she finished for him. "Like Margaret Martin. She thinks, 'They're not drowning on our beaches, so why borrow trouble?'"

Martin was Colorado's other Senator, longer serving, but up for re-election this cycle where Orin wasn't.

"She and Orin have hope to be on committee together. She's something of a mentor to both of us. Or was," said Janet. "She's very canny, very savvy, I'll give her that, but I had no idea how much she disliked me. For instance, she thinks that while every supportive spouse should make efforts in philanthropy, my choice of refugee charity is..." A sour taste in her mouth. "...unfortunate. She's even told Orin so, though he hasn't mentioned it to me."

Smart man, thought Verbenk, who wouldn't want to go up against this woman in a fair fight.

Her mouth quirked down, and she added, "She thinks that for the good of the Party, I should have staked my claim on a less controversial cause, like cancer or AIDS or veterans."

Legs crossed at the knee, she bounced one foot in frustration but fell silent, eyes focused on nothing and her brain obviously still fuming.

But he still didn't get the furor. Not yet. She'd not knocked down his door because people weren't as charitable as they should be. It was his opinion that everyone had the right to be selfish inside their own heads if they otherwise made good. Actions spoke louder than thoughts. Something bigger festered beneath this skin of outrage, and he'd use his intellect like a scalpel to find it.

"So why not cancer or AIDS or veterans?" he prodded. "Why child refugees? Why Love International?"

Janet took several swallows of her coffee, as if to refuel and/or measure her response. A luxury he never got, unfortunately for both of them.

"Well," she finally said, "it's the adults who are assholes, right? Full of hurt and anger and..." She looked Verbenk up and down. "...assorted ickiness, but kids are all promise and possibility. I mean, kids don't control where and when they're born." She raised a shoulder somberly. "Or who to, for that matter. They don't decide to be born where there's no access to vaccines or schools or, you know, safety from rocket fire. There are those in this world who are powerless, who have no one to defend or advocate for them. I am in a position to be that voice, and so I'm choosing to speak."

How polished. Verbenk rubbed his chin, wondering how much of that response was scripted and how much of her passion for the issue was genuine.

Pulling back in defense, "You *still* really think I'm that cold?" she asked. "This isn't just an 'issue' to me. And if it's not important to you—like it's not to Martin—you bastards are the cold ones. Jesus. Have you not seen the state of the world lately? I do not understand how anyone can look at these viral pictures of children, CHILDREN, fleeing for their lives—"

Her tone was scathing, and Verbenk braced himself. Like most people, he had seen the images of drowned refugee toddlers on the news—their cheeks still baby round, now caked with sand and never to move again with breath. He'd seen the dust-covered children in the back of ambulances. And he'd quickly changed the channel. Every time. And he wished she didn't know that.

"—and be such cowards," she finished, accusing the doctor with her stare.

It took conscious effort not to pull back in defense, to pull away from the heat of her—it was obvious now—100 percent genuine passion. Verbenk fumbled for excuses, and realized there was no use. She felt his shame, especially keen because he'd once felt like a refugee himself. Abandoned and friendless, landing on his uncle's foreign shores, which hadn't exactly been welcoming.

Still, Janet would have to forgive him for not instantly leaping off the couch and righting wrongs. Though refugees were one of many worthy causes in the world, she'd seen his life lately, right? He had his own shit to deal with.

"Oh, we adults all have our own shit," said Janet, seeming to retreat once more into her own space, into her own head. "Most adults are pure shit taped together with moral compromises. Always have been, probably always will be."

Pen poised, "You included?" he asked.

Janet blew a strand of hair out of her face that had become dislodged during her speech. In the unusual shadows of the office this early morning, her cheekbones

looked like beautifully sheathed weapons, but to his surprise, she shrugged reluctant agreement.

"More than I'd like," she said morosely, pressing her
fingers to the bridge of her nose. "More than I'd like. It all
goes back to the paradox: the damned if I do, damned if I
don't. I went with the TED Talk format for the event, and
they all think my youth is showing. If I'd stuck with a po-
dium, I'm sure they'd think I didn't have an original idea
in my pretty little head. And of course I only care about
these kids because I'm a woman, right?"

She weakly punched the leather with her closed fist.

And you don't have kids yet, he thought, which was
likely a whole other arena of judgment.

Her face flushed hot. "Oh, don't even step into that
steaming pile. Orin's sisters were there." She narrowed
her eyes. "After all these years, they still wish Orin had
married that Porter girl he went with ten years ago. The
bitch broke his fucking heart, of course, but she would
have been more *appropriate*. She married a cardiologist,
you know, and they have three boys. Three. And boys,
too, the show-offs."

Then she shooed that issue with her hands, as if she
couldn't get it away from her fast enough. "But it doesn't
matter. No matter what I do, I'll never be enough," she
said, spitting out that last word like rotten food. "It just
wasn't enough."

Finally! The point—and it was one of the decimal
variety. A bubble of satisfaction burst in his gut. It was
the money, always the money. Obviously raising less

than 200k for a cause just didn't cut the Grey Poupon among their political set. Those storied and monied people with whom Orin Buckmann of the famous Denver Buckmanns—politics went back in his family almost as far as the railroad wealth did—had grown up and still socialized.

"How much were you aiming for?" he asked, certain of his conclusion.

Janet sniffed and pretended to be very interested in the seam of his couch, which she was tracing with her finger. "Well, it is the money and it's not. That rumor of a refugee bill I mentioned?" she asked, her gaze only flicking toward him briefly. "We started that, Orin and I. We—*He* wants to introduce a refugee-family adoption bill this session, similar to the program run out of Canada."

The doctor winced, knowing how anything whiffing of the Great Socialist North would fare in the, as she described it, current political climate. He could imagine the internet comments now. If the Senator introduced such a bill, No. 1, Orin's support could take a big hit, but No. 2, did that kind of effort even stand a snowball's chance in hell? Was it worth the vulnerability of exposed neck?

"I know. Exactly," said Janet. "That's why Orin has said for months he'd gauge support before sponsoring it. But thanks to this stupid ability—" She held a finger to her temple, then threw up her hands, as if tossing away her telepathy. "—I knew that this event was it. The fundraiser was his litmus test."

"Shit," he whispered, commiserating.

"Shit is right," said Janet, calm and sad rather than fiery angry, a condition Verbenk actually found *more* concerning. "If I raised half a million, he would have moved forward to committee. A million and he'd have been one hundred percent ready to put his name on that legislation. But? But."

But $125,000. Pretty far off the mark. Verbenk deflated along with her. That sum could maybe buy one refugee family a starter home—in neighborhoods far away from this one, even outside the Denver metro area in general, anymore. With that kind of money, she would be trying to put out a conflagration with a thimble, and she was blaming herself for the failure.

"You can't do that," he soothed, placing his hand palm-down on the desk in her direction, as physically close as he dared get at the moment. "You can't—"

"Doesn't matter, because he won't do it now. He can't do it now, and I'm done," she declared, nodding her chin like a judge swinging a gavel to close a case. "I'm done with all of it. Fuck people. Screw needy children, who are probably just fucked-up adults in gestation. I'm never leaving the fucking house again."

And she timbered like a tree onto her side. Her shoes now off, she even pulled her knees up to her stomach, eyes glazed. On his couch.

"Um, you're in my house, not yours," Verbenk pointed out. "This is not a great long-term plan. Just hide at your doctor's? Just avoid your unavoidable power? When just yesterday, it seemed like we were engaging in some real thera..."

This time, it wasn't Janet's words that interrupted him, but instead her eyelids flying open, her spine springing back vertical like a Jill-in-the-box. Her expression... scared him. Her eyes were filled with real, honest terror and were locked on the window behind his desk chair.

The doctor whipped his head around to follow her gaze, expecting a monster, expecting horror. But seeing nothing. Just the curtains, just the big courtyard on the west side of the old house, its jigsaw flagstone path and its rose bushes, the thinning sunlight of a fall morning. Janet, on the other hand, was certainly seeing something Verbenk's mortal senses didn't, because now all the blood had drained from her face, and her knuckles were just as white, gripped like claws on her bare knees.

"No. No, no, nononononononono," she said. "Turn around. Turn around." Thinking Janet was speaking to him, Verbenk looked outside again, but, "Not you," she snapped. "*Her.*"

Then he watched as the gate to the side yard began to swing open and a familiar figure stepped one long, graceful leg through to the yard. Christine. He startled and looked at his watch. She wasn't scheduled until tomorrow, and it was still uncouthly early besides.

Puzzling, but hardly a reason to panic—this time of day, he knew the glint of sun on the window would hide them from outside view—but Janet was definitely panicking. Up from the sofa, she'd scurried deeper into the room like a wild animal. On her socked feet, she stood in a half-crouch, her hands over her ears, white-wide eyes pinballing around his study and looking for escape. Seizing on the room's only other exit, the door to his private quarters, Janet bolted toward it.

"Stop!" he called out, pointing, as if at a misbehaving dog. Her deep trespass into his mental privacy made his physical domain feel even more sacrosanct. Thankfully, she froze and pressed her back to the wall instead.

Verbenk peered back through the window. The intercom didn't buzz, but Christine hadn't reappeared. She was apparently standing out of direct sight on his door step. For some reason.

"What the fuck?" he asked, he pled, more to the universe than to Janet, because she wasn't listening. Whispering to herself, Janet was inching along the wall to the furthest corner of the room, where she then slid down into a roly-poly ball, arms around her knees. "Janet?"

Her eyes clenched shut, she hissed, "Don't tell her I'm here, that you're with someone! It would somehow get around. She's always hated me, but she saw that blurb about Love International this morning. Now she thinks I'm a witless Angelina wannabe."

Muttering confusion, he strode to the door and looked through the peephole. Christine's face was unexpectedly close, as was what looked through the fisheye like a giant pen, writing. She was using the door to write a note. Rather than let her finish, he opened it—although only two scant inches in order to obscure the room behind him, even if Janet was already cowering far out of sight.

"Oh!" Christine exclaimed, and the piece of paper drifted to the ground in her surprise. "Sorry," she said, bending down to pick it up. Wearing a jogging set of pale purple, with eye shadow to match and her blond hair pulled back in a ponytail, she smiled shyly, then awkwardly held up a static beauty-pageant wave. "Hi. Sorry. I wasn't... expecting you to be in the office already."

"Christine," he said. "Hello." Verbenk repositioned his hand on the edge of the door, trying to be casual, leaning against the frame.

"Sorry! Rather than bother you so early," she said, fluttering her fingers—which he noticed were somewhat bony, her gold rings loose beneath the knuckle, "I was leaving a note. I hope I'm not disturbing you?"

Verbenk made a point of not turning to check on Janet, respecting her request not to reveal the presence of a patient. Painting on cheerful expression that he hoped wasn't clownish, the doctor said, "No," followed by a cough. "This is just an unexpected surprise. How can I help you?"

"I just..." Christine's smile faded a degree. Oddly, she wasn't wearing lipstick, which she had never before been without. "Sorry, but since it's about twenty-four hours notice, I thought in writing might be best. I'm afraid I won't be making our appointment tomorrow."

"Oh?" he asked, heart calming at the routine nature of the request. Although, strange. She could have left a voicemail. The note strategy was definitely avoidant, and he wondered if he'd offended her—or rather, offended her, *too*, seeing how disgusting he was and all, according to his telepath.

Christine's dimples flashed, but weakly, and it seemed all the pretty women of his acquaintance were looking tired today. "I got an opportunity last minute to go out of town. On vacation. Um, Europe. For two weeks. Maybe longer."

"How wonderful! You and Doug both?" Behind the door, Verbenk was tapping his foot. He knew Christine and her husband had been fighting, so a vacation together—a romantic reconnection—was just the thing for a minor mid-life crisis.

"Right. Doug." A tightening at the corner of her eyes, though perhaps that was the morning sun.

Verbenk cocked his head. "Everything else OK?"

"Oh, yes," she said. "Just getting away, and sorry to bother. I should go. I have a million things to wrap up between now and then. Packing. Dropping the dog at the sitter. You know."

Nodding, he colored, remembering Janet's accusation about his observations and the image of Christine waiting for the back end of her dog to do its business. Verbenk couldn't help it if his keen observations were often prescient. Being insightful was part of the job. Then why did he feel ashamed?

"Getting away sounds like an excellent idea," he said. "Take some time to think about your next chapter. Your next phase, right?"

Still squinting in discomfort in the sun, she nodded. "Right. Right."

"So I'll next see you...?"

"I'll talk to you as soon as I get back," answered Christine, licking her lips, weight on her back foot, as if ready to bolt.

"Great! Have fun then!" he said with uncharacteristic jolliness, immediately feeling ridiculous.

"Sure. Sure, sure," Christine said over her shoulder, already on her way to the wrought-iron gate, which was taller than her and which she closed with another hurried little smile before flitting away as if she'd never been. Light as a ghost.

Verbenk shut the door.

A sheepish Janet was again on his couch, fanning herself with her hands, tears smudged into a damp wing at the corners of each eye. He pulled the heavy armchair closer to the couch—intervention distance—and sat down in it with his elbows on his knees.

"What was that, Janet?" he asked, his fingers entwined.

"I didn't vomit on your carpet from absorbing her angst," she said, her voice thin and exhausted but far from soft. "I didn't faint, like I almost did last night once or twice. You're welcome."

His eyebrows knit in confusion. "All because she... Christine hates you for some reason?" Was this all some kind of—

"No," Janet said, rubbing her forehead with both hands, hiding her face. "This is not about 'female drama' like you're thinking. She doesn't know me, just knows *of* me. She's also a Republican, so we're never going to be besties, but that's not why she overwhelms me. Why she consumes me."

"Fine." Pressing his hands together at his chin, earnest, Verbenk asked, "Then what *was* that, Janet?"

Posture caving in, she fell back against the cushions. "That's why either this ability goes away or *I* do, meaning I have to go into hiding. Last night was only two hundred people and I almost lost it." Her fingers pinching. "This close. I took six bathroom breaks. Orin was rather worried. But I regularly have to go to events with thousands of voters! The shield of a smile ain't gonna cut it. And yet here? I'm taken down by a woman—*one*—one woman who... who..."

But she couldn't finish. Janet was crying now, tracks already down her cheeks and a single tear hanging unattractively from the tip of her nose. He noticed that lightning quick, she reached up to remove it with a sniff. Overwhelmed himself, he flicked his eyes away so she didn't have to watch herself cry. He fell back into the chair with a thunk, not having a clue what to do about this very real, very painful problem.

Verbenk handed her the cube of Kleenex, and this time she took it.

He asked, "But you absorb my horrid thoughts without this kind of reaction. What is it about Christine then?" He looked once more toward the windows, thinking of his other patient, pretty in pink and as threatening as a kitten, to his mind. "This woman can overpower you single-handed, from a distance, with... what? Her mid-life crisis?"

Blowing her nose, "That's not what that is," she said, pointing toward the door that had divided her from this supposedly weaponized neighbor. "Angst. She's... like a black hole, sucking all the light out of the world, out of me, then refilling me with nothing. An overflowing nothing as heavy as lead. I can barely breathe."

Verbenk pulled back one corner of his mouth in thought, finding it difficult to understand what was physical sensation to Janet and what was metaphor. Thought was so unruly, non-linear, and according to Janet, voluminous that words didn't seem fully capable.

"And don't think you're not guilty of overwhelming me, too. That first day?" added Janet. "You almost had puke on your rug."

He looked at that carpet for a moment, silent, then "Hm," he said quietly. He slapped his thighs with his hands and stood to slowly walk the room, his hands in his pockets.

"I have to ask why, you know? Why me?" said Janet, sniffing sadly. She picked at the tissue, her knees knocked together. "I don't want to be avoiding my husband this morning, but I'm unable to stop obsessing about what he hasn't told me, and his thoughts are about nothing else."

Verbenk noted, "Hence this morning's surprise visit."

"He's off to D.C. again until the weekend, takes off in about an hour." Janet sniffed. "I hate being like this. I hate this!" She shook her petite fists, ineffectively shaking some sense into the world. "This is not how my life is supposed to go. I've never before felt so betrayed and confused and utterly... powerless."

Before he could stop himself, one sharp, "Heh," left Verbenk's mouth, startling him. Startling her, too, eyes wide. "Oh. You didn't mean it that way?" he asked, his mind immediately turning back to pulpy, spandexed superheroes. "Come on. You can see why that's funny."

"I suppose," said Janet, wiping her eyes again, too morose for humor.

"Powerless?" He waved his hands around, as if to make the connection for her. "And you have a superpower?"

"Yes, yes," she said, still unamused. "I get it."

Verbenk, on the other hand, was snagged. A punny accident, certainly, but.... perhaps this train of thought was a valid one.

"Actually," he said, leaning against his office's wall of books in order to better think, "telepathy is one of the strongest powers in comics' universe." Because did they not build an entire series around the powerful telepath Professor X? Did the Professor not train, as Verbenk had seen just last night—this was just too perfect—a young female telepath to harness her powers?

Jean Grey! Marvel Girl, but made modern in Janet. How marvelous. The doctor felt inspiration tingling and... was it *hope* rising? A pure, childish hope spurred by a pure, childish love. That was it. His comics had the answer.

"But you do realize, right, that you're *not* powerless in this situation?" he asked, searching her face for the first time with this superhero frame of reference, looking for signs of magic or destiny or... something. Instead she blew her nose, threw the tissue on the coffee table, then stuck her tongue out at him, but Verbenk paid no mind, continuing, "You literally have a power, one no one else has. If you could just shift your perspective to what you could *do*—"

"Mwa. Ha. Ha," she deadpanned. She was looking at her hands, palm-up in her lap, shaking just slightly. He guessed she was assessing if her pills had taken effect. "Sorry," she said, "but I'm not really feeling up to taking over the world, or whatever telepaths do in your nostalgic little stories."

But excited, Verbenk strode to the office window. Four-color, pointillist comic memories and extrapolations riffling through his brain like a flipbook. It was whimsical, certainly, but he talked the budding idea out, out loud, saying, "Almost without fail, what people do in the comic-book universe when they're struck with supernatural abilities is, one, become overwhelmed by them." Verbenk waved a hand to take in her appearance.

Rubbing her eyes had made them puffy, and there was that vessel on her neck, pulsing mad. A hero without her make-up. "Check," Janet said.

Verbenk continued, "They say, 'Oh, why me? Whatever shall I do?'"

"I do not sound like that," she muttered. "I will never sound like that."

"They stumble a few times, they fall, but then they... bloom into it," he said. Grinning, he clapped his hands.

"They embrace it, embody it, accept the sacrifice for the greater benefit. They *really* change the world, *really* save people."

"But for *fake*," Janet stressed, followed by a snort of absolute ridicule. "You're talking about fiction, and this is the big idea you have to fix my life?"

Verbenk didn't spare a care for her derision, asking, "Is there really any other way out? I don't think you have a choice about going back to your old life, so this is where we are."

He was pacing now, wondering why he hadn't thought of this before. His point of view had been too rigid, obviously. Too academic, as if when his uncle had hidden his comics, he'd destroyed young Verbenk's creativity. For years, he'd been handcuffed by textbooks and case studies and professionalism. However, science fiction and fantasy stories could be seen as philosophy in fictional form, an author's way of positing what-ifs and what-thens. Well, what-if was right now, then comics' what-thens were as good a place as any to start.

With this new perspective, the doctor's brain was already off and away, drawing the future. Picturing himself as the young superhero's mentor, remembering the training sessions the Professor had set up for his young mutants/Supers. Talk about redemption! Music-from-*Rocky*-level redemption.

"A training montage?" she asked. "Oh, gods."

Verbenk continued pacing, his chin-stroking unperturbed. They'd need more distance to play with than what his office provided or his large backyard with its lonely pool, which he paid to have cleaned and never used. They'd need a field trip for their next session, to go somewhere like a park and—

"No!" Janet sputtered. He turned to see the woman tightening her arms around herself. "A public park? Have you not been listening? I don't want to be exposed like that, like a lightning rod, and for strangers? I'm trying to avoid thoughts, not seek them out." She was panicking at the mere thought of the experiment, her knuckles white and chest heaving. "I didn't ask for this, you know, and you're just pushing, pushing. You keep pushing me."

Verbenk's heart wrenched. In the face of all she'd been experiencing, of course she was exhausted and confused, her already warped conception of self pulled until it was paper thin, almost transparent.

"Hey. Hey," he soothed, holding his hand out into the Persian-carpeted space between them. He was feeling too good to even step toward the mistake of underestimating a vulnerable woman again, and instead he used the comfort of his words, of his thoughts. "Before you say no, think about it."

They stared at one another, her eyes wide and teary. He saw her chin quiver, and she quickly covered the offensive display of weakness with her hand and looked away.

"This is about learning to control your powers so they don't control you," he continued, doing his best to effuse kindness. "You know you can't keep on going like this, pretending nothing's changed. You *can't* not leave your house again, not if you love your job and your life as much as you say you do."

"I do!" said Janet, teary, nodding emphatically despite. Her voice an unsure whisper, she continued, "I really do."

"Then you're going to have to try something to take control of your power eventually, right?" said Verbenk, consciously relaxing his shoulders and taking his own emotions down a few notches. "But not this very moment. Not right now."

The kernel of a plan felt like gas in Verbenk's tank, like solid ground under his feet. This session had worked for him like mental Viagra, and he was so pleased. Not merely for himself, though. Also because that energy gave him comfort to share, comfort by proxy.

"Oh, thank god," she whispered, anticipating the meditation to come by slumping over to lay with head upon pillow, forearm blindfolding her eyes. One foot carelessly draped onto the floor.

The doctor leaned against the warm window pane and began to hear the roar of the ocean, as giddy as a boy on the boardwalk with a pocket full of change.

4

Three days later, Verbenk saw his work-in-progress life ending in the oncoming lanes of Colfax. As they jumped the center-median curb, the tires of Janet's luxury SUV jolted beneath his ass, and he squealed, clung to his seat-belt and bargained with the universe: *Not yet!*

"Sorry!" Janet shouted, yanking the steering wheel and returning them to asphalt with another jounce. She glanced in the rear-view mirror at the double arc of tire tracks she'd carved in the narrow, grassed median and winced, wiping sweat off her brow.

"What was that?!" Verbenk demanded, eyes wide in bladder-testing terror. Kicking himself, because in all the cajoling and planning that led up to today's field test of her abilities, he'd forgotten the minor matter of transportation safety. Note to self: *Never again get into a car with a crazy woma*— He caught himself. *I mean, an unstable person.*

Despite his hasty correction, Janet cut him with her eyes, recovering some of her haught and her composure. "I... I got overwhelmed. I'm sorry."

"But... but..." A simple sorry didn't seem sufficient, not when he'd almost *died*. Verbenk's rattled mind could not move on from visions of white airbags deploying in slow motion, the imagined pain of femurs crushing against the dashboard, the horror of dying with a life not yet fit for the obituary he craved.

Now back in her lane, "Oh, calm down," Janet said. A visible shiver travelled from her neck, down her shoulders and into her thankfully now wheel-gripping hands. "Something like a broken femur would be nothing compared to what I feel passing that minefield."

Swallowing with obvious distaste, she flicked her head back toward the scene of the grass-mauling, right in front of the of National Jewish Health hospital campus. Known for its respiratory medicine, he could still see a banner on one of the red-brick buildings reading, "Breathe easier!"

Verbenk was sure as hell trying, but his teeth chattered with now-unneeded adrenaline.

"Oh, you'll survive—this car can handle a little curb— but there's a swarm of people back there who won't," Janet said. "Gunshot wounds, childbirth, cancer. Some actively dying, some soon enough, and so many of them in pain and in need and stacked on eight floors of... Well." She reached under her sunglasses to wipe at her eyes—until Verbenk's glare demanded her hand return to 2 p.m. "Hospitals are the worst."

"This is why you need to learn to control your power," he said in frustration.

"Pfft," she huffed. "Let it go." Janet drummed her fingers nervously on the steering wheel, now waiting to turn right. "Or shall we talk about why *you* don't have a driver's license?"

"No," he pouted. Verbenk hugged himself, his body still thankfully whole.

She shrugged, saying, "Suit yourself," and entered the road circling Washington Park, the site they'd agreed upon for today's field test of her abilities. Covering several city blocks, Wash Park was a massive swath of landscaped nature cut across by trails and surrounded by Victorian cottages. Cottages, however, probably no longer applied here in the 21st Century, because most of the homes had been mansioned, now boasting new wings larger than their original floor plans, their former carriage houses remodeled into three-car garages or pool houses.

As the scenery passed, Verbenk thought it amusing, how they'd traveled from one enclave of the modern gentry to another. In fact, if he ever managed to solve Janet, he should drop a few of his business cards in this neighborhood to drum up more clients. Sure to be tons of easy Lonelys and depressives.

"A whole park full of them, I'm sure," muttered Janet as she turned into one of the larger lots, pulling the parking brake as if the poor thing had wronged her.

"Not at all," he enthused, hopefully tamping down her nerves, because it had taken all his effort to convince her to participate today. She hadn't left the house since their last formal session, except to go to his and insist he stop leaving her voicemail messages. His number appearing multiple times on her phone's missed-call list had angered her, as if he were evidence of a crime, which had in turn hurt him.

But Janet's case of unexpected telepathy had taken on a destined-quest sort of urgency for him, thanks in part to his late-night binge-reading of a huge chunk of the *X-Men* series, which had not been an inexpensive purchase. He'd amazed and delighted the young punk at the comics store. He would not, could not, fail now. In fact, the planning of this outing had been the first time since he was... fired—the word was even mentally jagged—that he'd felt his dedication to his job rekindling. The job that for a solid decade had consumed all his energy and all his time, leaving little room for a personal life, and he hadn't cared.

Now he'd begun to feel that if he just had his work again, could just solve this one magic case, maybe the rest of the pieces would come closer together. He wanted to be whole again, to go back in time, because it turned out falling apart was downright exhausting.

"I can relate," muttered Janet.

"Look," he soothed, taking in the outdoors himself, hopefully calming them both. "It's the perfect day, just as you demanded."

Now safely immobile in the parking lot, the sun shone warm on his shoulder through the window. A breeze was pushing fluffy clouds with noticeable speed through the blue sky, and the trees in the distance were mottled yellow and green, changing color for the season. As he'd hoped, their parking lot was only sparsely populated with cars. School was in session until the afternoon, and therefore the park was not yet full of screaming miniature tyrants on too little Ritalin.

Janet had insisted: No crowds, especially of kids. She'd also insisted: No hangovers, and Verbenk had complied on that count, too.

"Still," she said, grimacing. "This is not going to be fun."

Although he was nervous, fun is exactly what it sounded like to Verbenk, probably because of all the reading he'd done in the last few days. The similarities were striking. For instance, Jean Gray also had strawberry hair, which was drawn as wild as flames around her face, though Jean (later the Phoenix, later the Dark Phoenix, and wow, he'd become one of those comics geeks) was always depicted in green spandex rather than Janet's black. Jean had even once absorbed the traumatic emotions of a dying friend. (She was likely also not a fan of hospitals.) With such significant parallels, the storyline was the closest thing he was going to get to a case study of Janet's exact condition.

And he was going to help a real-life Jean Grey!

Janet muttered, "I'm not, I'm not, I'm *not* Jean Grey."

"Come on, you're not ready?" he asked, turning in his seat to better gauge her mood. "You're not at all excited, or at least, happy to perhaps get some answers?"

She was obviously Status: Not Ready, saying, "You're assuming there are answers." Though they'd arrived at their destination, Janet had made no move to get out of the car. Instead she pressed her back flat to the leather seat, still holding the wheel, arms locked. Today she was pale but resolute, her hair pulled back into a tight bun of some sort, her legs encased in black exercise leggings. (Her workout clothes were almost as omnipresent as the woman's coffee.)

The outfit was part of the camouflage, because apparently she and Verbenk were "jogging buddies." As Janet had explained on the ride over, she'd labeled this unusual field trip in her All-Important Schedule (shared with her husband and staff) as time with a "jogging buddy." Verbenk handled the term with quotes, distastefully, as if the desire to exercise might be contagious. Apparently all Janet's sessions with him had been logged as runs in her calendar to cover up her therapy sessions.

Such bending over backwards to cover her tracks. The telepathy was that big of a secret, as was he. She was that insecure... concerned about maintaining the image of normalcy. That unwilling to let her new power affect her, to the point that she'd failed to even consider a basic inventory of her telepathic abilities until now, almost two months into the experience.

"Hey, I've been handling it," Janet said, leaning her head back, exposing her pale neck, "the best I can. I could do without you if I had to. I'm fine."

"Ahem," he said, scratching his cheek, mentally broadcasting, *just like you almost handled your way right into a massive, multi-car accident.*

"And he's not letting it go," said Janet in a sing-song voice.

Well, it was hard not to dwell on, you know, *nearly dying*, but Verbenk silently promised he had only one last entreaty, which was, "Until you have some control, please say you'll use a driver or something. Seriously."

After all, they had *staff*, which included a smattering of clean-scrubbed secretaries, aides and interns. Even some security, burly dudes who seemed to do little else but stand around behind sunglasses. Certainly there was someone on the payroll to chauffeur a car.

"No." Janet shook her head vehemently. "We do have someone in security who drives Orin, but I can't stand him anymore."

"Why is that?" asked Verbenk, because he knew she wouldn't otherwise elaborate. Though she'd become more open to the therapeutic process, new information still only escaped her kicking and screaming.

"Just a personality conflict," she evaded, staring out the window of the car at the park's lake, which a family of ducks were gently stirring as they swam.

Verbenk cocked his head. "Of what type?"

"One you'll get too much enjoyment out of, I think." Janet began gathering her things, zipping her phone into one of the hidden pockets of her sporty jacket, grabbing a plastic bottle of water and shoving it into a canvas tote bag. (NPR pledge-drive freebie, he noted.) About as excited as a wet rag, she asked, "Ready to get going?"

She popped open the car door, but he held up a finger to stop her. His instincts sensed meat. "Nope," he said. "The driver is obviously a part of your telepathy, a condition which you have come to me to treat. Tell me."

Her signature eye roll. "Always pushing. Fine." One leg already heading for the parking lot, gripping the door handle as if for a getaway, Janet scrunched her mouth into a paler pink before she answered, "If you must know, he... he does Kegels."

The doctor snorted. "Excuse me? You mean, Kegel exercises?"

She sighed in pent-up exasperation. "Yes! Continuously while he's driving. Squeeze, release, squeeze, release. You know, training to last longer during sex?" Color in her cheeks, Janet look to Verbenk for confirmation he understood. "Well, I just can't listen to him. I don't want to *feel* it with him. Squeezing, counting. Especially after I caught a glimpse that when he's at home... no. I can't say."

He playfully pushed her shoulder. "Tell me!"

"You sure you want to know?" Janet's nose wrinkled in mingled mirth and distaste. "Maybe you don't want the vision seared in your mind like it is in mine."

But of course, Verbenk loved secrets and intimate details, all those dramatic, juicy bits. A person's secrets were usually their most interesting stories or traits, carefully hidden behind the bland masks they donned for one another—all the same, all utterly boring. Secrets were the candy in the piñata.

"Tell me," he insisted, because after swimming in his—often murky gutter of a—mind, did she really think she could shock?

"I suppose not," she answered the unspoken question, looking to the ducks as if for guidance. "If you must know, at home he uses a washcloth as weight on his..." She stumbled, becoming uncomfortable with her descriptive gestures, letting her hands fall. "And he... flexes with it, to strengthen the muscles, and times how long he can manage it."

"He does... penis push-ups?" the doctor asked, forcing out the words past the guffaw boiling up his throat. "With a towel?" Then he was unable to say more, choked by the humor.

"No, a washcloth," she said. Then her embarrassment broke, Verbenk's mood literally infectious, and she forced out through laughter, "He's working his way up to the towel."

For a brief moment, together, Janet and Verbenk dissolved into giggles and dissolved the tension built up between them by their arguments about this day, this experiment. Quick as blinking, though—quick as catching their breath and remembering one another—the situation reasserted itself and the car descended again into thick, uncomfortable silence. They each faced forward, staring out at the ducks while the engine ticked itself into silence. Unlikely car-fellows, strangely coexisting in the world outside his office.

"OK, then," she said, finally sliding down from the SUV. "Let's get this over with."

Verbenk tumbled after like a dog behind his master, slamming the unfamiliar car door, and gripping tight to his notebook and pen. "So the first step of the plan," he said, "we'll need to head up to the—"

"Soccer field," provided Janet, ripping the words from his mouth. And frankly, ripping away a bit of his excitement and pride. She could at least let him speak his plans aloud, but she was already in motion, striding away, her healthy legs eating up the ground, and tossed back, "It's not my fault I'm a mind reader."

"Doesn't mean you have to rain on my parade," he grumbled under his breath before calling out, "Hey, wait up!"

Without turning or acknowledging him, Janet's pace slowed minutely as she left the path and cut away from the lake and the ornamental flower garden toward the field.

As he approached the running path surrounding the park, trying to catch up to Janet, a sporty-assed woman ran between them behind a leashed border collie, her ponytail of blonde curls bouncing. Enjoying having a novel new ass to admire—only fantasy—and feeling fresh air in his lungs, Verbenk realized how isolated he'd become. Even the slight climb up a grassy knoll to the soccer field was more of an effort for the doctor than it should have been. The loafers he'd become accustomed to wearing every day around the house were loose and unsuited to the task. He felt a little loose and unsuited himself and tucked his shirt into his pants where it had come loose, vulnerable all over.

Thankfully, the doctor saw when he summited that tiny hill that the timing aspect of the plan seemed to have panned. Though swarming with colorful jerseys and screaming parents every weekend, the soccer field today was a mostly empty expanse bracketed with un-netted goals of painted metal. Their only company was an un-leashed dog and its owner packing up their game of fetch near the opposite-side 'penalty area'—one of many new bits of soccer vocabulary Verbenk had googled up in his research, because he'd never been allowed to experience the American childhood bonding ritual of team sports. Sports were "nothing but psycho-sexual exercises of in-grouping and dominance" in the Verbenk home, where books and facts and keeping your damn feelings to your-self were the household gods.

Near a bench at the hill's ridge, Janet placed her keys and tote bag on the ground, then her hands on her hips, and scanned the park in all directions. To the north of the lake, a few adults sat on benches around a set of swings and slides on which a small tribe of children played, their shrieks somewhat muted from this far away. Otherwise, Verbenk saw only rustling trees on the soccer fields' far side, and heard nothing but the muffled noise of traffic. He fiddled with his notebook, eager to begin.

"So there are several levels of this experiment I'd like to try," he said over the mild wind. He cleared his throat, attempted to reign in the enthusiasm he always felt when tackling a promising experiment. "The first of which is putting an exact number on your telepathy's range. I thought of the soccer field because—"

"It has a built-in ruler for measurement. I get it," said Janet as she began to stretch, holding first one sneaker and then the other behind her to lengthen her thigh muscles. "I see it all, doc."

He watched the foreign process in curiosity, while he explained anyway, unwilling to forego the excitement of explanation. "Goal line to goal line is a hundred meters, so we're looking at three hundred feet of space to test your capabilities." The penalty-box line was 50 feet from the goal, followed by the center line out at 150. "And this line, where I'll stand," he said, pointing to the goal only a few feet away from where they stood, "will be our ground zero."

Janet said, "So you'll stay here near the bench? Probably wise." Looking his body up and down, she was probably feeling his elevated heartbeat, the tightness around the waistband of his pants, and she was definitely judging him. "You'll have a place to rest."

She was also pressing one arm across her body with the other now, then switched, then began to shake out her neck.

"While you do what?" he asked, reminding his bitter self that she was a good twenty years his junior. "Run a marathon? Why are you stretching?"

Janet shrugged, jogging in place now on the balls of her feet. "I was thinking line sprints. You have all those test lines in your head for my range, so I thought—"

"Line sprints?" he interrupted, always two thoughts behind this tsunami of a woman.

Cue eye roll. "It's a fitness drill," Janet said. "You go out to that first line and back, then out to the further one and back, then... Oh, never mind." His frozen, open-mouthed incredulity must have been enough response, because she let her gesturing hand fall, let her heels again touch the ground. Deflating. "I just wanted to get my heart rate up while we do this silly little exercise. I haven't had any time lately to actually run."

"Because you've been 'running' to my office instead," said Verbenk, feeling himself catch up. With a fake run on her calendar today, she'd have no time or excuse for a real one. The expert two-bird-stoning was so very female.

She squinted, sneered. "Shut up."

"Is that level of... exertion necessary? I was thinking about a simple, leisurely stroll out until you can't read me anymore, but..." *Wait.* Click. "This is really about your mocha calories, isn't it?" Verbenk said, waving his pen at her like a wand. "That's what the, um, line sprints are about."

"Shut. Up." Janet kicked her sneakers toes in the grass, like the petulant teenage daughter he never had, and crossed her arms, which were clad like her legs in thin black fitness material. Not meeting his gaze, which meant he'd hit the mark.

Oh, he knew his housewives and how they thought. "That's the price of your little act of rebellion." He failed to suppress a quick grin of pleasure. "Not so fun having someone reading your mind, huh?"

Her mood dark and scowling, she said, "There is nothing wrong with trying to control how you visually present yourself to the world, especially in politics." Pursing her lips, she added, "Besides, Orin's on a diet right now, too, actually."

Verbenk could believe that. Orin Buckmann was a polished man, a controlled man, a glowingly healthy man. He was probably cutting his afternoon snack from 20 raw almonds down to 12 or some shit because he'd seen a trace of chin flab from a particular camera angle. He would be a man who counted his almonds.

"Seriously. Shut up," Janet said, but Verbenk saw her face had fallen into disbelief rather than anger. "But also seriously, how *do* you do that?"

He was right about the counting. He knew it! His cheeks flushed with pride.

But then she continued, "How can you be so prescient about some things and so fucking dense about everything else?" Thereby popping his bubble, letting Verbenk feel the slime of himself drip down his bones to pool in his stupid, too-loose loafers. Insult to injury, she added, "And I have to say, doc: The tassels on those shoes are so 1986."

"Should I ask Orin what would look more appropriate?" he snapped before he could stop himself.

Finger raised in warning, "If I have to tell you to shut up one more time..."

The doctor settled for a huff out of his nose in response. Janet was allowed to lash out, he'd decided, and he was not. While he may have been feeling exposed out here in public, Janet literally was—and he suspected she was far more nervous than her practiced face let on. He was ready to grant her some serious slack.

"How about we establish your range," he offered, "and then you can jog around the park for the second part of the experiment? Because once we understand the distance component, it's vital for me to see the telepathy in action—" *On someone besides myself.* "—and expose you to different stimuli, thereby hopefully giving you strategies to cope better with your telepathy in your daily life."

"Oh, goodie," she deadpanned. "Stimuli."

In order to hold his tongue, Verbenk pressed it in frustration against the roof of his mouth and instead followed through with the other promise that had cinched Janet's participation: that there would be somewhere safe to which she could retreat. He went to that safe place now. He wiped his mind clean of himself and breathed the ocean.

The sand. The sun. The living water. There was the beach—in fact, the very California public beach he remembered from his childhood—on a day as sunny as this one, a place without pressure or hurry. There was his chubby butt in the sand, chubby thighs before him, the surf licking his chubby toes. There was the bathing suit of his childhood, his mother with a towel in her ratty canvas tote. Inhale, waves tickle, little boy giggles. Exhale, shushing back out to the cool dark sea.

Verbenk breathed deep. The child laughed. His mother laughed, too. The world moved around them, but all was serene. He heard Janet exhale in what sounded like calm resolve.

"That's your mom?" asked Janet—causing the doctor to blink his eyes open in surprise. Janet was breathing easier now, again shaking out like an athlete on the hunter-green grass, flapping her hands at the wrists and then her feet at the ankles.

The sharp sun of the present afternoon dazed him. He felt a bit... small and disoriented, as if his big, adult self was now standing next to his patient in the same small bathing trunks. The addition of the personal memory to the scene—the maternal guest appearance—had been unexpected.

"Yeah. We used to go to the beach a lot." He cleared his throat, flipping open the notebook to the pencil-lined chart he'd constructed for the purpose of their experiment. Memories of his mother were rare for Verbenk, who had long learned to keep her consciously unconscious in a blowtorch-sealed vault buried in his psyche.

"She left? Or is she dead?" asked Janet, freezing in mid shake. "Oh, gods. She left in some tragic way." A tremor ran its way down her spine, which she held abnormally straight and tight, making her a half inch taller than usual. "Put it away. Put it away."

"Sorry! Sorry. Of course," he said, completely rattled by this left-field mutation of his perfectly planned day. *That's over*, he told himself. Old news, nothing to see here, folks, move along. Though an unfamiliar breeze still ruffled his mental landscape, he pushed that old pain back into the soup of repression, where it belonged right now.

Janet must have been holding her breath. Her mouth a perfect O, she now deflated, the tension retreated, and she melted back to her normal height.

"Not here," said Janet. "Not today. You promised—"

"And I will." He found himself shaking out his shoulders in unconscious mirroring, and instantly stopped. Verbenk was no athlete—he was wearing khakis, for fuck's sake, with pleats—so he pushed his glasses up his nose and returned his attention to the experiment. To the patient, who was more important than him and his tragic past. Delving into his childhood comics had just knocked something loose. That's all.

"There. Put away. Feeling more ready now?" he asked, far too jovially, perhaps over-correcting for his overshare.

No longer a bouncing, calorie-burn-primed bundle of energy, Janet had lost her buoyancy, and now stood still and planted, as if the ground might shift unexpectedly. Stepping up to the starting goal line, she said, "I tell you, I'm done with this radical honesty shit. Some things need to stay private for damn good reasons, you know?"

"Sure?" he said, feeling his face crinkle in confusion. Physically feeling his damn wrinkles. Age did that, made you feel all the things you couldn't control. Like women. Like everything.

"And that makes me as ready to get away from you as I'll ever be," said Janet. "So in order to start this precious little test of yours, I should just go...?" She pointed out toward the opposite goal with dual finger guns. "How far?"

Consulting his notes, Verbenk coughed and re-centered himself in the plan. The record of his affirmation looped in his head: *You will prove yourself and your worthiness anew, you will prove yourself and your worthiness anew....*

"Number one, I'd like to see how your experience changes at different distances," he said, smoothing out the page. "So first, let's play with the volume of your telepathy. I know standing this close to someone can be overwhelmingly loud, so just walk out to the minimum possible distance at which you would feel comfortable interacting with me. Or," he corrected, knowing where he fit in her hierarchy of favorite people and not relishing another insult, "any random person."

First filling up with air, as if diving into a pool, Janet obeyed—only because she wanted to, he knew, rather than out of any sense of respect or authority usually present between himself and his patients. He'd take it. Despite all his instincts against, he was beginning to understand that pride was sometimes optional if all you really cared about was getting shit done.

As she walked, Verbenk tapped his pen against the notebook paper, a bundle of nerves. He looked at his watch. Man, the field was much larger in person than in his imagination. It took a long time for someone to walk when you were standing still, he thought, keeping his eyes on Janet's measured strides, hips rolling left then right like boom-badda-boom-badda-boom, like a sexy metronome.

And only then did he see his range-testing plan did have one tiny flaw: He was going to have to watch her go, and it was such a pretty picture. Her back, her waist, how the thin jacket ended in flattering curve above her ass. If there were extra mocha pounds on her, he couldn't point out where. He wondered if weight was also something her husband policed in terms of image, or if the idea for additional exercise was hers alone.

"Stop looking at my butt," shouted Janet, tossing the words over her shoulder.

Startling, Verbenk almost dropped his pen, but then mentally defended, *Merely involuntary appreciation!* Then to himself, *Think of baseball. Think of any-damn-thing else.* But—damn butt—it was her that had brought up the subject of weight and appearances.

At this point Janet had passed the penalty box of the soccer field, a distance of about 25 feet, which was apparently the minimum length of pole with which she'd prefer to poke him. There she turned around and again faced him, today across grass rather than carpet, her weight shifted all to one sneaker and her arms crossed.

Without prompting, "I'll have you know, staying in shape is just part of politics these days," she seethed, lecturing him. "That is, if it ever wasn't. It's all about symbols. Fat politicians make people think they're wasteful and greedy at work, with taxpayer money, as well as at home. And fat women, well, aren't allowed anywhere." Hand on hip, she asked, "Like I can singlehandedly change the importance of image in politics? Or antiquated views about women as window dressing or trophies?"

Needing to raise his voice a level across the distance, flicking pen against paper, Verbenk said, "Interesting. I didn't suggest you could."

Janet snorted. "Wow, that's a very textbook shrink response from a man who was inspired to today's experiment by some ancient *comic book*."

"Hardly ancient," he muttered softly, but then allowed his offense to trail off into neutrality. She had the Jean Grey pass. Instead, he waggled his head in satisfaction and began to look at the success of the experiment in question. No matter the origin of his plan, it was working—or beginning to. Making notations in his chart, he asked, "So you're happier out there. Now if I think of a number between one and one hundred?"

He closed his eyes—hard, as if that made a difference—and did his best to randomize a number for her to pluck from his mind. Squinting one eye open, in the distance Verbenk saw Janet cock her head, tuning her antenna.

"Thirty-three," she said quickly, with the attitude of the star student he was sure she'd once been. "That's such cake. You did say minimum comfort distance."

"Very good," he said, happily marking down this first landmark on the budding map of her telepathy he was creating. Whatever was inside that 25-foot radius around Janet could then be considered in the Danger Zone, capable of overwhelming her.

Janet waited off in the distance, tapping her toe. "Again, we're talking minimum," she repeated. "How about I get a little farther from 'danger,' eh? Should I go out until I can't hear you at all?"

"Of course, of course," he muttered, scribbling as she turned without further prompting and began to walk farther out, this time more plodding and less boom-badda. He squinted into the pale, autumn sun and screened his eyes to see her go, adding darkly, "By all means, flee from my detested presence."

"Don't judge me," she tossed over her shoulder. "You'd flee yourself, too, if you could."

His only answer was a shrug. Sad, but true enough. He would never have used such words, and certainly would never have admitted that embarrassing point to another soul, but—deep breath—this was not about him.

Janet was about to cross the goal-box line at this point and showed no signs of stopping. Forty-five feet, then fifty. His nerves tingled and he stepped foot to foot, shuffling. He wondered how far could she possible go—dear gods, he'd thought 50 would be on her extreme end, but still she walked—and he decided to think of a number, to broadcast that number as if he were a radio station set to one frequency. Testing her.

"Eighty-two!" Janet yelled toward him without stopping, proud to prove wrong his doubts.

"Wow," he said to no one but himself, because thanks to the strength of this superpower, which he was reclassifying as more super than expected, he would have had to shout for Janet to hear him. Though the distance was impressing him, he had thankfully had a contingency plan. He yelled, "And since you're farther, we'll need to switch to—"

"Yeah, yeah," Janet said—or at least, Verbenk thought she did. Her words were muffled, facing the wrong direction, his hearing not what it once was, and he was unsure if she could now clearly read in his mind what he'd like to convey.

"Your phone!" he shouted.

She'd stopped about 20 feet farther on—for a total of 75 feet—before again turning to face him. Her form was getting noticeably smaller thanks to perspective, but he could see Janet zip into her jacket pocket and emerge with her phone. Rather than calling him directly, however, she began to click around the screen, her thumbs moving madly. Breeze ruffling his pant legs, Verbenk gave her a moment.

Which stretched into two moments, then three. So, "Janet?" he called, making her name rise to a point. "Janet?"

"One minute," she yelled, one hand fumbling with a Bluetooth headset at her ear, the other still fiddling away on the phone. "I have to answer this."

He took his own mobile—an old iPhone, too *small* for fashion now, proving he'd never understand fashion—out of his pocket. In comparison, Janet's big screen was the size of the old black-and-white portable television they'd had in the kitchen. He used to carry the thing over to his mom in bed on her bad days, when she said the sheets were swampy. Like glue. He'd pictured the quicksand he'd seen in cartoons while he played with action figures in the other room.

Shut up, Derek, he thought, flicking his gaze up causally to see if Janet was responding to the memory—she had not, was still texting away—and realized the door to the past wasn't so easy to close. He pictured himself blow-torching the mother vault back into repression, where it belonged.

Only then did his phone ring.

He answered, "What are you doing over there that's so damn import—"

"I told you to put the angst away, didn't I?" said Janet, tough, all business. Looking super business-y with that headset, very power-lunching executive.

"Sorry." He winced, but then his eyebrows met in confused conference on his forehead. "Wait. You can—?"

"Hear you?" Janet sighed into the mic, her voice strangely intimate in his ear over the phone line, closer than she'd ever gotten to him in real life. "Just the... feeling. I've always said that emotions seem to broadcast particularly strong, haven't I? Yes, your angst is faint and more manageable from here," she added, looking away over her shoulder. "And, well, maybe you're actually being helpful." She began walking backward farther away, phone pressed to her ear. "We're now calibrating for emotions."

He hoped she was calibrating for his frustration, too, softly saying, "Glad my grief is helpful to you and all." Still, he made a note: 25-75 feet they could perhaps call the Annoyance Zone, where Janet could still pick up on the broadcast of other people's minds, but retained a degree of control.

Then Verbenk waited for Janet to settle; after pausing a moment at one distance, she took two more steps, paused, then one more. He could have sworn she sniffed the air in between, as if for the scent of him, and he admitted: He was wounded. Which must have *also* had a faint transmission, because she took even one step more, finally landing about two-thirds of the way to the center line.

The doctor emitted a "grah" of frustration from deep in his throat, a noise that he must have learned from Janet herself, but said nothing more. Thought nothing more. Instead, he filled the back of his head with the rhythmic pull of the tides.

"OK. OK, then. Look at this!" she finally said over the line, stretching her arms ferociously over her head, like a woman waking up for the second time that day. "I think I'm finally free out here. It's kind of nice to have an unopposed opinion of my own. I feel… so light."

"Congratulations. Looks like about a hundred feet," said Verbenk, who though he still found this whole grand and comic and comical idea promising as hell, would not have described his own feelings as freedom. More like a tether between them had snapped. More like without her in the picture, he might slip away, blow away.

Just like the ribbon of yellow leaves tossed around in the wind over the swath of grass between them, but he used his notes to keep himself grounded, writing down this third realm of telepathic sensation as the Emotional Zone, where distinct thoughts were out of range, but extreme emotions carried. They could call anything from there outward the Quiet Zone, he supposed.

"A hundred feet doesn't sound like a lot of distance," she said, "but I suppose my house isn't more than this from public areas, making it almost totally exposed in one way or another."

The doctor also pictured the blueprint of her massive house, or as much of it as he was aware of, having never been inside. A colonial number with white columns and red brick, a porch stretching the length of the wide curbside approach, and a neighborhood path running directly along the back property line. No wonder she liked his house more. In hers, she would indeed have few places to hide.

Then Verbenk took the image of that series of rings—Danger, Annoyance, Emotional and Quiet zones—and overlaid those dimensions on the average grocery store. Then a traffic jam or a business meeting or a ski slope or a movie theater. Or the Ellie Caulkins Opera House on the night of big charity gala. Or a hospital, lest he forget. (He'd never forget. Fear did that.)

A lot of people fit in 100 feet. All those constant radar incomings. All those people, striding around the world like blaring radios, broadcasting their dirty laundry in the form of scary, incoherent noise and random sensory information. Verbenk got a little overwhelmed just in the imagining, but wonderfully, Janet seemed utterly unperturbed. Wonderfully, because her state of mind, not his, was the important thing.

He was happy to see her attitude—perpetually unwilling—was even slightly improved. "I think we're finally clear, but send me another number," she commanded, and he watched the foreshortened woman rub her hands together like a catcher, as if this were all a game. "Just to be sure."

Hey, he thought, she was at least playing ball. Concentrating with all his might, Verbenk repeated the randomization process, settling on the number 17. "I've got it," he said into the phone, but the background hiss of transmission was the only answer on the line for several beats. "Janet?"

Looking up, he saw that if she cocked her head any more to the side, tuning her antenna, it might just roll off her head. Closing his eyes to better focus, he painted the number with neon in his head, traced it over and over again, like a kid spelling his name in sparkler: 17.

With a sigh of relief, "Nope," she said. "Nothing." Then even more joyously, "Nothing at all. Out here, it's just me and the sun and the breeze and..." Smooth, unlined face up to the sky for a moment, she then snorted and seemed to return to earth, glancing to her left. "...and the scent of pot being smoked somewhere nearby."

He laughed. Verbenk could picture her cute nose wrinkle. Janet had told him during the car ride over that she'd thrown out the borrowed Xanax after only one dose, and he couldn't imagine her ever being loose enough to be interested in marijuana. The woman didn't even enjoy a good healthy drink—or at least, not as much as Verbenk would prefer she did, since she'd been judgmentally keeping tracking of *his* drinking for weeks now.

Goodie-goodie do-gooder, and he forever mal. Malpracticing, malfunctioning. He wondered if the pot smoker might share—*Hey, man, mind if I hang with you?*—and he was so happy he could think such things without their ridiculousness being instantly mocked.

"From where?" he asked, his nose and senses perking. He drew his concentric circles around Janet now—red, orange, yellow and green—as if she were the center of a permanent radar. As if Verbenk were her radar operator. "Ah," he said. "There's the offender."

Sure enough. A lanky, young man emerged from the shelter of the trees to the east, a likely little hidey-hole for a quick toke of marijuana, which while now legal to consume, was not technically legal to consume in public places. Stoners rarely cared about technicalities.

"That kid who was here before with his dog," Janet said, whipping back to face Verbenk, but then stopping with her foot extended toward him. She jerked again toward the kid, then back halfway, then made a decision to avoid both and faced the park. She began to jog in place, as if that were her typical resting position. "Sit down on the bench. Pretend we're not together. He'll wonder what we're doing. "

"What does it matter what he thin—?"

"I don't want to take any chances of being recognized. With you. Doing this." Apparently unable to keep up with the faux jogging, her posture was suddenly oh-so-casual: one hand in a jacket pocket, the other touching her Blue-tooth, likely to clearly project that she wasn't crazy, wasn't just talking to herself out here on the field. Playing the role, he thought, of a woman on a run stopping to take a call from a co-worker, from a friend, from the nanny.

All for show, because Verbenk thought it unlikely the kid, for one, took a deep interest in Congressional politics or, for two, had anything in his head other than the Grateful Dead's multi-colored dancing bears, truckin' up to Buffalo. Which made the stoner rather perfect, really.

"Calm down, Janet," the doctor said, settling himself on the bench of wood and metal, the latter quite chilly against his arm, but the rest welcome. He'd never be in shape again, would he? What was the point? In this little show, he was apparently to play the role of the old, duck-feeding man, decrepit and friendless and sad and easily invisible. But, "That kid gives no shits about us, I promise," he continued. "Although I'll have you confirm that for me in just a moment. Did you bring the binoculars, like I asked?"

"What? I mean, yes. They're in the tote bag there," she said as the doctor reached for the binoculars and trained them on the kid.

The dog, a mutt shepherd of some kind, rather runty, was off leash, trotting happily three feet in front of his person. They were crossing the width of the soccer field, ambling toward the main body of the park, a good—Verbenk squinted—100-plus feet away from the telepath and sticking to a parallel path to her. No immediate threat.

"You mean we're moving on to the aforementioned stimuli? Do I have to?" whined Janet, though her tone remained teeth-clenched, fake cheerful. "What? Did this Jean person in the original comic like hanging out with stoners or something?"

"Well, those issues did publish in the 1960s," he joked, bringing the binoculars up and focusing on the kid.

Rough blond cheek fuzz—probably 18 or 19 years old at most—he was wearing slouchy, fraying, holey cargo pants, and had a goofy smile. A smile like he knew something the world didn't. He was the type of ruffian it was often hard to identify in Denver: homeless or hipster?

Either way, "A great first subject," Verbenk surmised. He quickly flicked the binocs up to follow a V of geese when the kid happened to glance his direction. Just a bird watcher. Nothing to see here.

Janet stomped a foot ineffectively in the cushy grass. "Is this absolutely necessary?"

"When a neighborhood Republican sends you melting into a corner," he answered, "then yes, I think so. I think you can handle some distant, mild exposure to a harmless stoner."

Meanwhile, Verbenk monitored the young man, who'd paused to light up a cigarette and toss the ball for the dog, who was off in streak back toward the trees. The kid smoked and waited, and the doctor took the time to explain the next steps of the experiment.

"The plan here is based on immersion therapy," he said, talking over Janet's dramatic sigh. "The idea is to create a hierarchy of discomfort. Hence the range-mapping we just did. Then you progress to exposing a client first to smaller and then to larger discomforts, using a relaxation exercise to maintain calm when necessary, and the hope is that they're eventually able—on their own—to handle their trauma, their phobia, their—"

"Superpowers?" asked Janet, poking him with her sarcasm again.

Momentarily lowering the binoculars, he pinched the bridge of his nose and answered, "Don't be ridiculous."

"Oh, it feels ridiculous," she said. "Mentally eavesdropping in a fucking public park feels pretty fucking weird."

"You curse a lot when you're nervous. Or frightened," he said, again watching through the lenses. The kid was on the move again, so they needed to act now or lose this subject for good. "Are you frightened, Janet?"

"He's coming closer!" hissed Janet, cupping her a hand around her ear mic and mouth, flashing suspicious eyes toward the kid.

"That's the point," he answered, mimicking her whisper into the phone, pinched between his ear and shoulder. "But he is our *minor* stimuli. He's stoned! Happy as a clam, and likely totally harmless." Verbenk bit his lip, hoping his threat assessment of this first subject was correct. "Now, just let him pass without moving away, if you can, remembering that you're not trapped."

"You don't know who this man is," said Janet, retreating into her teenager's huff. With the binoculars, he had an up-close and personal view of her face now, despite the distance, and was able to see every tug of nerves under her forced expression of calm. That woman's moods were an iceberg: Only a seeming harmless amount of Janet was visible, but she was no less dangerous for that.

Making tranquil, calming hand gestures that he knew she couldn't see—perhaps calming himself—he answered, "No, but I know you, and you can handle him. I also know that all you have to do is come back within comfort range of me, and I'll have that relaxation exercise the therapy talks about. The—"

"Ocean," they said in unison, despite their mental separation.

Janet was nodding now, her jaw set. "All right. All right."

As if acting on the universe's command, the young stoner's path took a turn closer as he approached the park. He cut diagonal across the downhill toward the jogging path, crossing the 100-foot boundary into the Emotional Zone.

Verbenk's chest rose along with his blood pressure, as if he were watching a race. One on which he'd bet a decent sum of money—or in this case, all of his pride and hope and self-respect, which in sum total, wasn't much but was also everything he had. "Anything?" he asked nervously. "If he's emoting anything strong, you should be able to...?"

She shrugged, angling her body away from the kid, keeping her back to him as he sloped her direction. "He's... hungry. I can tell that from here for sure," she said as the kid tossed the ball again, exhaling a stream of smoke.

He snorted. Having toked a few in his day, Verbenk could have guessed that much. But the kid was moving closer with his loose, lanky stride, unknowingly drifting deeper into her unseen web.

"Oh, stoned off his gourd," she unnecessarily whispered as he passed about 50 feet behind her. "There are apparently food trucks around the corner. His name is Matt. He moved to Colorado for the legal weed, of course, from..."

Curious and concerned, Verbenk shifted the binoculars back to Janet's face. Her cheeks seemed to be visibly thinning while he watched, then began to bloom an unhealthy red. Her red flag. "Nope. Nope," she said and began to jog backwards farther into the soccer field, stumbling once and recovering.

"What? What is it?" Repositioning on the bench, eyes glued to the binocs, "Try to stay," he urged. The forgotten notebook on his lap closed, sandwiched around his pen. "He'll be in range for only a few moments. And remember: He can't hurt you. He can't literally hurt you in any way."

Janet seemed frozen in an awkward position, though he could tell she was trying to obey. His lip bite bit in harder, causing pain. Then, "Nope," she repeated and took to her toes, jogging along the center line a few paces, even though the young stoner was still in motion back toward the parking lot, already getting farther rather than closer.

Flabbergasted, Verbenk asked, "What could that kid have done?" while watching the stoner approach a shabby white sedan. The kid was smiling, looked like even singing to himself. How was he not the ideal candidate?

"More like what was done to him. Just... trust me," Janet said, slowing down again after a few yards, strawberry ponytail swinging to a stop. "Bad memories have a habit of bobbing up in flashes and half-conscious surges—no matter how calm and normal people look on the outside. Poor boy. Poor, poor boy." In extreme close-up, he saw her mouth pull down at the corners, lips pressed in anger. "The stepfather," she seethed.

Verbenk's face similarly compressed, knowing how tender her heart was to children. Of all the first subjects, *dammit.*

"Discomfort is part of the exercise, remember. Are you breathing?" he asked, shifting his weight forward, lifting himself a millimeter from the seat. "Or I will come over there and—"

But her nostrils flared wide, her chest rose. "Stay there. I'm fine. Some people just should not be parents, but I'm fine," she said, rapidly nodding, rapidly speaking. "Immersion therapy, huh? Well, I didn't drown. I guess I survived it."

His ass fell back onto the bench in relief, though he tried to keep that relief out of his voice. "I had no doubts you would."

With a rueful laugh, Janet said, "Oh, you may have had lots, but from here, I wouldn't know, would I?"

Verbenk swallowed hard, and looked down, opening the notebook and running his finger over last night's planning. Instructions: Challenge, reassure and praise, then inch up the challenge. "You're doing great, Janet," he said into the phone in his best coach's voice, thinking of the reassuring presence of Professor X. "Gold star. Now, try to keep in mind when you feel caged in: It's an open park. You can't be trapped, and I'm right over here."

One hand to her temple, facing him again across the distance since no one was now there to see her do so, she said, "So we can't just adjourn early?"

"Of course not!" he answered in the most cheerful tone he could muster. "Do you call *one* dip in a pool immersion? I know you're enjoying your privacy out there at the moment, but..." He paused to watch Janet stomp her foot ineffectually in the cushy grass, and said, "But this is necessary. I don't think you can communicate with your constituents and donors or colleagues via cell phone and binoculars, no?"

Janet sucked her teeth in annoyance, and the sound sucked at his ear. "No. Fine, fine, fine," she said, sliding her phone into a pocket and heading for the hill down to the park, muttering.

"Now," he said, settling back on the bench, enjoying his perch, "let me find you another subject. They won't all be stoners with dark pasts." At least, Verbenk hoped so.

"Take your time," she replied, smoothing back her hair and heading toward the jogging path, using her sneaker toes as brakes on the descent. Constantly rotating her head right and left as if checking for eavesdroppers. "At least I can get my heart rate up while I wait for instructions."

With that, she settled into a slow but steady jog. Verbenk, on the other hand, scanned with the binoculars and begged the universe: *Please, let there be someone easy.* Someone who would make this careful plan pan.

Once a group of three women and two dogs cast him suspicious looks from the jogging path, and he made a point of watching the trees for a moment. Again playing birdwatcher, he tracked a few taking flight, made some notes and gave the binocs a break for a few minutes. No one wanted the cops called. He should have brought some bread to feed the birds, he thought, thereby making himself entirely old and invisible.

But even without the binocs' magnification, the park and the lake unfolded before him like a diorama. Like a miniature Christmas village, everything manageable and cheerier from far away, a world in which he was just a viewer. He took his own advice to relax and breath, closing his eyes into his ocean meditation.

But the fall wind now held a chill, and so the beach's sky was gray and lidded, the noise of the surf rough. Also rough was the tricolored Mexican blanket on his shoulders, his knobby knees pulled up under at their campsite among the dunes, which you could get away with for a night or two on the off season. He was older in the meditation now, about the age he was right before...

Stopitstopitstopitstopitstopit.

Very dangerous territory there. Verbenk cleared his throat, realigned his brain with a sharp shake and forced the waves to behave. He painted the sky blue, calmed, then put the binoculars back to his eyes.

"There," he said, seizing upon two promising new subjects about 200 feet from where Janet currently jogged along the path, heading toward the tennis courts. "In the ornamental garden," he continued, watching a pair of elderly women strolling the paths that X-ed through raised beds of late blooming flowers, which reminded Verbenk of embroidery. "Just head down toward the flowers."

He pointed forward and to the left, using his whole arm so Janet could follow the gesture even from a distance were she to look back. But she didn't, changing course seamlessly, plowing away at her jog.

Verbenk casually returned to his tom-peeping surveillance. One of the elderly women was hunched over a cane. A quite recreational cane, he thought, ending in four, rubber-bumpered prongs, as if for uneven terrain. She was pear-shaped, lumpy, her pants likely of the elastic-waistband variety. The other's spine had yielded less to the slope of time, and she clutched her handbag in front of her non-existent belly, the purse and her dress both floral.

"At that wrought-iron fence, you'll be about… seventy-five feet away, FYI," he said. "Just two harmless seniors."

Between the regular puff-puff-breathe, puff-puff-breathe of Janet running that direction, she replied, "You said that about the kid."

However, she still stopped obediently a good distance from the fence, slowing to a halt and looking back at him, their eyes meeting through the glass of the binoculars across the gulf. Hers wide and scared and making clear she'd hold him responsible for any more mishaps.

Carefully now, she stepped forward toward the fence, past which a hedge blocked her visibility of the garden— though from higher up, Verbenk's was unobstructed. A double-blind test, then. Each of her steps was careful, testing the waters, her hands held subtly out as if for balance. Janet was pinging her radar for strong emotions, he was sure.

At the fence, "OK, yeah. I hear them vaguely," she said.

Nervous, Verbenk saw that the women were now edging into Janet's Annoyance Zone, meaning Janet had to intentionally tune in, but she was likely able to sense their minds.

Sure enough, Janet added, "Lots of Latin names for flowers now. Memories of people I don't know."

The women were rounding a far bed in the garden and turned to hobble back in his and Janet's direction. With their careful amble, they would do the work of gradually turning up the volume on this experiment for him. He literally crossed his fingers, a game he hadn't believed in even as a boy, because neither crossed fingers nor star-wishing ever worked for him the way other kids claimed it did.

"Breathe. Stay calm," he said as the women came closer, closer.

"They're heading toward me, aren't they?" asked Janet, who was tilting her head, reluctantly tuning.

Focusing in the lenses, he assured her, "Yes, but they're laughing. Probably old friends, out for a walk."

"Yes, that's true," she admitted. "Very old friends, but man, they're achy. Everything hurts." And Janet rubbed her right hip, grimacing.

Verbenk shifted the binoculars back and saw that the caned woman had stopped, and though still smiling, she was also massaging her right hip, talking wide-mouthed, obviously complaining about the trials of old age. He then moved the lenses back and forth between the senior and Janet, who despite being separated by age and obstacles and distance, were moving in perfect accord, like syn-chronized dancers. He was slightly awed, the transmis-sion even more magical from this godlike perspective.

"She's in remission from cancer, you know," said Janet, strain audible in her voice. "Not the hip-replacement woman, but the skinnier one."

Shit. Fear began to chill Verbenk's stomach, but he took his cues from Janet and stayed calm. "Remission is good news, though, right?"

"If you mean she's not terminal, sure. Or at least, no more so than the rest of us."

The doctor scrutinized her tone, her body language. "But you're—"

"I'm OK. I'm breathing."

Then the women were again inching closer. Seriously. Inches at a time. Verbenk gave his binocular arm a rest and looked at his watch. The seniors halted at a sign planted in front of one of the flower beds. Suddenly, they faced one another, and they were hugging, shoulders bouncing up and down. Laughing again, Verbenk assumed, but sudden hyperventilation on the line contradicted that assumption. Lenses back up to his eyes in a flash, his gaze rocketed to Janet.

She was bent almost double, one hand on the waist-high fence. Struggling for breath, "Oh, Jesus. I told you so!" she shout-whispered in anger. "She's being evicted! The woman who just survived cancer is losing her home of thirty years to the bank. And her friend already lives in her son's basement and can't help her." He watched Janet's knees knock toward one another, growing watery. "Her hair hasn't even fully grown back and she's lost every—"

"Back away," Verbenk said, cursing silently. People were forced from their homes every day in the world, and not just by war in far-off places in North Africa and the Middle East. He understood that truth, but did they need to go through their tragedies here and now and so close to his poor telepath? "Turn around. You can always get away. I'm coming."

He shot to his feet, throwing the notebook in the tote— then he dropped his phone in the gravel underneath the bench and cursed, aloud this time. Fumbling the dusty, now more-scratched phone to his ear, he caught Janet in mid-sentence, saying, "—didn't want to do this. You know, there's a reason we all don't tell one another every little thing on our minds, doc! Some of that shit is best kept, you to deal with yours and me to deal with mine, and I need to stay *out* of it."

She'd sprinted away a good 100 feet from the garden by this time—though she was still well out of range of Verbenk himself—and she paced right and left on the jogging path beside the tennis courts, right and left, muttering. The doctor slipped down the hill from the soccer field in his loafers, unsteady, as if walking on water.

"I'm coming," he huffed, the tote bag on his shoulder wedged beneath his armpit.

This was his moment. By design, they'd known that the possibility of overwhelm was high, and he'd therefore built in a release valve: him. As he scurried nearer, Verbenk pushed down his own panic, drowning it in her favorite meditation. He was a portable island of sun, sand

and surf tug-boating toward a woman in need of rescue, while she continued ranting into his ear.

"...not everything *should* be available for popular consumption. I know what it feels like to have every bit of my life visible to public most of the time," she said. "You make fun of me, but I don't think you understand how privacy is *protection* in my world."

She stopped for only a beat to draw in more air, more ammunition. "When you control your image, you control your exposure, and..."

He shuffled as quickly as he could on the jogging path now. Then suddenly, as if he'd crossed some invisible line, he knew the moment when the ocean reached Janet. He could hear it in the change in her breathing, which began to follow the rhythm of the waves. Verbenk stopped in a patch of grass near the lake in order to close his eyes and better concentrate, letting the image and the sensations lap at Janet's toes. The searing sun was easy to imagine, since his strangled, red face felt much like sunburn, and this time, even more details emerged. Music—Motown hits, his mom's favorite—played on a portable boombox perched in a drift.

After a moment of silence, he risked opening his eyes, which were for some reason full of tears. Janet stood facing him across the distance, in her Annoyance Zone. A gust of wind ruffled his pant legs, ruffled the several patches of grass alongside the winding paths between him and Janet. The shriek of a child on the nearby playground made both of them cringe, grating across their taught nerves.

And the silence between them stretched, until, "This is how it's supposed to go, remember?" he said, as soothing as he could. "It's supposed to be hard, and then it's supposed to get easier."

She'd started shaking her head, mouth pursed, before he'd even finished talking. "No. Like I said, I'm done. And not only for today," said Janet, focusing solely on the ground, on her feet. "I'm done with humanity. They're just too fucking hard on me."

"Come on, one more try," Verbenk begged, knowing that no matter how Herculean the persuasion, he would not be able to convince Janet to undertake anything on this scale again, and he strangely felt that something final would have occurred if they failed here today. A gavel falling, the verdict upon his talent as a doctor made—but the plan hadn't failed *yet*. "Please," he said. "I *know* you can do this, and hey, just look at that. Some nice, low-hanging-fruit kind of stimuli."

Another shriek, and since she was back within telepathy distance of the doctor, Janet turned toward his idea before he could even point toward the gravel and slides and swings of the nearby playground. A kid in shorts and a cute little hoodie was hanging from the monkey bars, swinging for that next rung. Another child popped from the end of a spiraling tube of a slide, like a tennis ball from an automatic server. Four young girls were jumping rope on the nearby pavement, braids bouncing, hopping foot to foot in a rhythm as regular as drums.

Wholesome, he thought, though he was now very leery of his own assessments. *Stupid cancer*. He shifted the tote bag on his shoulder.

Deadly serious, Janet said, "Oh, I don't think so," and she crossed her arms, tucking her finger tips beneath her elbows, he assumed for the warmth. The light was thinning even in midafternoon, these autumn days growing so short. Their window was closing.

Trying not to beg, Verbenk said, "I thought you loved kids. All that pure potential and stuff."

"I do. In the abstract," said Janet, stalling, kicking her feet. "In the flesh, however... Well, they'll be as disappointing as their parents, won't they?" And with her voice lowered to a near whisper, "I don't want them to be as horrible as their parents. Let me keep something pure, please?"

Watching her across this distance, he resorted to mental entreaty. *Please. We need to try this. Therapy is by nature uncomfortable, but discomfort heralds change, and you need change, don't you?* And then Verbenk called back to mind her breakdown in his office, painted the memory in Kodachrome clarity. Janet scurrying like a wild animal for safety, her hands claws, her wide eyes.

She clutched one hand to her throat now, the other to her belly. "No," she repeated with authority. "Don't."

Closer than she was to the playground, the doctor could see a portly young woman with dark hair sitting on one of the surrounding benches, a double-wide stroller for two infants beside her. Another adult was alternating chatting with the woman and cooing into the baby-mobile.

"Looks like there's twins over there!" he said enthusiastically. "Everyone loves twins, and the mom is sure to be—"

"Exhausted and irritable and suffering from clogged milk ducts? Yes," said Janet, who had by now kicked herself to the water's edge, placing a corner of lake and about 40 feet between her and Verbenk.

Eyebrows raised in hope, "Also happy, I'm sure, right?" he asked. "Glowing and all that."

"Even worse." With that Janet grabbed a rock from the ground and threw it into the water. Not in a childhood-nostalgia attempt at skipping, but instead like a baseball pitcher, creating a violent splash of cold water and a wet plunk.

Startling, "What the hell?" he asked.

"Really? You haven't put this together yet?" she asked, and even with space between them, Verbenk saw her jaw working with emotions he couldn't quite place. "Ridiculous. You're keen enough to pick up on my mochas or to guess that my husband counts his almonds, but you haven't even caught a whiff that you're on sensitive ground here?"

She sighed, long and deep and angry and resigned. And sad. Kids don't decide where they're born, she'd once said. *Or who to*, she'd added ominously.

Shit. A very dark lightbulb went off in the doctor's mind. The many medical tests she'd assured him she'd had in the last year. Janet's dedication to Love International, and her heartbreak about toddlers dying on beaches. Orin's ex-girlfriend's three boys. Click. Verbenk watched his brilliant plan, brilliantly melting into a puddle of should've-known-better mess on the pavement.

"You and Orin can't have kids," he said, the words plunking between them like that thrown rock, and the sweat on Verbenk's forehead and back became suddenly lake-cold. "Infertility?"

Thick with sarcasm and emotion, "Bingo! You can be a dense mother fucker," said her voice into his ear.

And his inner voice added, *stupid mother fucker stupid stupid*. His first reaction was a defense: She was so young! Of course he hadn't guessed. His mind hadn't been primed to the subject. His second was heartbreak: Oh, she was so very young. And she'd been hiding this pain from him for so long.

"You were hiding that from me?" he asked.

"Age doesn't matter," she said, ignoring the audible question. Her sneakers viciously trod back and forth at the lake's edge. "Primary ovarian insufficiency is the final diagnosis. Usually happens before age 40. We found out late last year, though they didn't have that name then. The name was more recent." She snorted, then added, "Insufficient."

Verbenk from a few weeks ago would not have expected a patient-kept secret to hit him this hard. But today, his breath knocked out. The news was perhaps not as leveling as his firing had been, close, but unlike him, she hadn't deserved her loss. She'd not made the bed for her tragedy to sleep in. She didn't deserve her fate. He swallowed too heavily, knowing the last thing she needed was the sadness he felt boiling its way up his chest.

Goddamn. Goddamn.

"Hey! I don't need your pity. I don't want your fucking pity." Her ferocity caused a bird in a nearby tree to startle and wing away to a safer home. For once seemingly oblivious to the potential audience around them, she pointed at Verbenk across the lake, which was rippling now with wind. "*That* pity. Right *there*. Stop it," she said, placing her hands over her ears—which only amplified her voice to the headset mic, and the words rung in his ears, too: "Stop it!"

But he couldn't get the evil irony out of his head. For a man, marrying younger was supposed to have the benefit of fresh eggs, of lengthening a man's reproductive window. Surely that stereotype was one Janet unearthed often in other people's minds. And now...?

"Now I'm useless, literally just a pretty face," Janet completed. "Yes, please dwell on that fact *longer* in my presence, you dense asshole. Stop!"

Then a baby's cry from the playground, and Verbenk saw the new mom holding one of the twins, bouncing him or her with one arm while the other pushed the carriage away from them along the path, toward a different parking lot. He tried to refocus. He was the release valve, the safety net. Sherman's words appeared in his brain: *We are men of science. Pull it together and don't be an embarrassment.* He huffed a few Lamaze breaths, his mouth a tight O.

"All right, OK," he said, hoping that the words would prompt more words, hopefully the right ones. "We can handle this. Together."

For a moment, she, too, calmed a few degrees. Verbenk cleared his throat, suppressed and tried to pretend this water's edge was a different one. He conjured the caw of seagulls. The beach's images ran faster than usual in his shaken mind, a short-attention-span MTV splicing of pictures and sensations. Tiny bubbles in the water receding around his feet, sucking him toward the deep. Sunscreen and peanut-butter sandwiches and towels and blankets and sunbathing. His mother sunbathing, sleeping, her face turned away in cheekboned profile. Sleeping and unmoving, for far too long, as she did far too often. He'd once been so worried, he'd held his mom's cracked compact mirror under her nose to check if she was still breathing.

She had been. That time. He'd been about 9 years old.

No. *No*, Verbenk thought, squeezing every muscle of his face in effort. Not now!

"What…?" he heard Janet ask breathlessly over the line.

He tried to shift gears and go back to how the beach used to be for him and Janet, that very first day: inhale the wave up the beach, and exhale the water and waste and fear and pain out. But it seemed he was too late to change the momentum. The pressurized details exploded.

When his mom overdosed later, he'd been 11 and there had been vomit blocking her airway. The paramedic had swiped the goop out with two gloved fingers as young Derek watched frozen in fear, still clutching the house phone with which he'd dialed 911. Later he sat in a police station until his uncle arrived on the first flight to California to take them both home. Derek to Sherman's home, his mom directly to the treatment center, from which she never emerged. The place they said she'd be on suicide watch, so he—oh, he'd been so small, so worried—could end his years-long personal watch. The place that had failed her, and him.

All of his secret history, released into the wild. All of this in the space of one breath, maybe two. Veritable seconds, but seconds that couldn't be taken back. He blinked, stunned, waiting.

"Suicide?!" Janet demanded, again off the handle. Her fists were clenched at her side like a rocket about to take off. Verbenk clenched, too. Everything. "*This* is the moment you want to think about your mother's suicide?!"

He looked left and right. Even a few parents over on the playground had their heads turned in his and Janet's direction, but she seemed too worked up to care.

"Hey, now," he defended, his voice sharp with tears. He'd guarded that memory so vigilantly, had constructed his entire life as defense against it. He'd studied and learned and worked and impressed and acted and done everything right, in order to make that memory not matter. Not define him. "It's not like I wanted to," he added. "It's not like I chose to show you that—"

She laughed, wild and unhinged. The sound seemed as loud to his one naked ear as in the one attached to the phone. "No wonder you're so fucked up! And fucked up about women, in particular, because they all leave you, right? So don't get attached. No wonder you've never had an actual relationship but instead a long series of furtive, shameful fucks you pass off as a dating life."

Her bile-drenched tone of deft psychological analysis rankled. "Hey, I've had relation—"

But Janet talked right over his, well, lies. "Come on. With that kind of history, no wonder you have all that angst. Depression runs in the family, doesn't it? Why, of all the doctors on earth, did I have to come to you?"

And that was it: the end of his patience. Anger Hulk-ed up inside of Verbenk, green and large, making him grow two inches taller.

"Hey!" he repeated yet again, because of all the patients who could have come to his door, he'd had the misfortune of her, too. "For someone who hates psychiatry, you sure like to armchair it," he said, spitting the words, and he would have spat literally had he the saliva, but his mouth was dry.

"Oh, I have to be better at the job than *you* are," Janet then accused, gesticulating wildly with both hands. "This was a stupid idea from a stupid man. I should have known better. I should never have agreed to this stupid, comical 'experiment'—" Dramatic air quotes there, her lips curled. "—of yours. I should have turned tail and run from your office that first day."

The, to his mind, patience of a saint he'd displayed out of deference for what Janet was experiencing snapped. In Verbenk's head, the peace treaty of Jean Grey burst into flames and boiled his blood. Janet's tote bag fell from his shoulder into his hand, heavy, and he briefly thought it would make an ideal projectile. He could just swing and release, right at Janet's pretty and currently red and contorted face.

Then more anger, because he had no space or privacy. She'd already have seen that violent thought, too. And— of course, as always, because he knew her well enough by now—she'd turn it back against him somehow, even though thoughts weren't actions. Even if no person was the sum of their unpredictable, turbulent thoughts.

"This is what you do with your power, isn't it?" Verbenk screamed back at her, his screech unmanly—part of him *hoping* to get her recognized now. "You make your distress other people's fault, saying how horrible everyone is—while claiming so righteously that helping people is your life's fucking purpose? Hypocrite!" Verbenk backed away, trying to pull himself out of her web of power. His heel met a rock, his ankle wobbled, but he kept his feet and kept moving in reverse. "You judge your poor driver, poor Christine. And me! Always turning it back on me. *I'm* disgusting. *I'm* broken."

Hands on hips, "Well, aren't you?" she tossed back.

"I'm your doctor, dammit!" he said, stomping in his frustration at his voice breaking, ruining his rant. "And… and you didn't think to even mention your struggle with infertility in our sessions?" Because infertility in and of itself was an intense experience that justifiably sent many people—male and female—to seek professional help. That alone would have been enough, telepathy be damned.

After several snorts of anger, Janet tried to bring herself under control. He watched, part fascinated and part disgusted, as she tried to reassemble her public mask. She smoothed her hair, pulled down her jacket, and turned away from him with her hand on her headset, as if it were not too late to pretend she was talking to someone not present instead of him.

"As I've told Orin, it's no one's business but ours," said Janet, much more quietly, but no less rageful. "Because if this gets out, it will define me. You realize that? For the rest of my life, I'll be known, number one, as a powerful man's wife and, number two, as that poor barren woman. Pity for the rest of my life. Everything attributed to that for the rest of my fucking life. No, thank you!"

"Right," he tossed back. "Because everything is about appearances."

"Fuck you," said Janet, her sneer dramatic enough to reach a theater's back rows. "Now, I'm going home. You? You can call a fucking Lyft for yourself, because I cannot..." She paused to press one fist against her lips. "I cannot be near you right now."

"Fine." Verbenk judged the distance between them. Oh, she could still hear him, if barely and vaguely. Good. "That's fine by me. But call a Lyft for yourself, too, because..."

In his left hand, he held up the tote bag carrying her binoculars and water—and car keys—out at a right angle. In the direction of the water. Janet spun back toward him, eyes sparking fury. Tilting her head desperately for more information, she also leaned forward, priming herself like the runner she was.

"Are you serious?" she seethed, needing to ask for confirmation only because he'd edged out of her range of absolute certainty. "You wouldn't."

Still stumbling backward, knowing he'd need as much of a head start as he could get to make an escape, he yelled, "Oh, I will, because *you shouldn't be driving!*"

And then without further thought, he flung the tote bag into the lake. The NPR logo spun in the air in slow motion. Fear and anger and exhilaration swirled inside Verbenk. The bag fell with a slap. Wet spread over the ivory fabric for a moment before it covered the bag completely and pulled it down into the darkness.

Briefly victorious, Verbenk pressed the button on his phone to disconnect.

"You bastard!" Janet shouted, her voice so muffled and far now that the connection had been severed. She took to her toes and began quickly eating up the arc of grass between them.

Verbenk turned tail and took off like his life depended on it. He fell as much as propelled himself over the grass, through the parking lot, over gravel and pavement and sidewalk. Past park-goers gawking at his haphazard, sweaty flight, and toward the street—any of the streets—bordering the park.

He turned once to see Janet still at the lake's edge, facing the water, both hands holding her head, but he shambled on, pulling farther and farther out of her power's range, falling out of her sphere and wanting to drop directly off the face of the earth.

5

By the time Verbenk caught his breath in the back of the hired car, he knew that whatever Janet's sins, she was right. About all of it. The cover of his anger evaporated and something darker poured in to take its place. A flash-bang grenade holding several decades' worth of tears threatened to explode behind his Adam's apple and take over his whole head.

"As fast as you can, please," he'd said to the driver, who was thankfully a brusque and unquestioning woman, likely correctly reading the depths of her passenger's scowl. And then he slumped against the window, world blurring by outside—and even inside, his eyes full of tears—and the realizations coming as fast and thick and piercing as a volley of medieval arrows.

How did he not see it? How did he not at least sense this large of a submerged-iceberg issue? The reel of Verbenk and Janet's time together played back in his mind, and subtext filled itself like comic-book speech bubbles. "Some people should not be parents" morphed into "yet some people that should be parents never will." He swallowed too heavily, straining his throat, and since the vault was now open, the memories were unchained and fierce—and included those words of his uncle's he'd never, ever forgotten, even if he hadn't consciously thought of them in years.

"She was always the black sheep, of course," he'd overheard Sherman say to a colleague at the post-funeral reception, the two men tucked into a windowed corner in the mourning room, dust suspended in a sunbeam, brandy snifters in hand. "Always wild, doing whatever the other kids did. Always susceptible," he continued, then lowered his voice even further to whisper, "I mean, to tell the truth, she really wasn't the type who should have had children."

And unseen, young Derek slipped out of the room through the panty hose and dress-pant legs up to his new room, which smelled of cleaning products, and he decided that he'd never talk about his mother again. He'd never let it affect him, because being susceptible was obviously a nasty, weak thing to be.

Commanding himself not to cry until he got home, the old Derek now slipped even further down the car seat as his own life washed over him. It was true all right: He was broken. His mom had broken him first, and now here came Janet, pulling him into her orbit only to drive a knife between his ribs. As if his firing hadn't made the message clear, here it was again: Women will decimate you if given half a chance.

Or, no, not women. It was him, wasn't it? The only common component in these heart-slayings was him. Freud himself couldn't have fixed this *mal*formed mess of masculinity he'd become.

His ragged inhale caught the driver's attention. Their eyes met through the rear-view mirror and quickly rico-cheted apart, and he felt the car speed up. She obviously wanted rid of him before he dissolved in her backseat, and the doctor didn't blame her.

You are not depressed. You are regrouping. Oh, the de-lusion, but he sniffed himself together for a few minutes longer, because in addition to feeling this overwhelming pain, he understood fully that a furious woman was—or soon would be—on his trail, and Verbenk had started to cobble together another plan. This one far more dark and desperate.

"How much can I give you to go fifteen over the speed limit here?" he asked the driver, already adding a big tip via his phone.

When the Lyft came to stop at the curb of his house, Verbenk bolted from the backseat full of frenzied pur-pose, because what was going on right now in his head could not, should not, *would not* be shared.

The front gate swung open with a metallic whine; he locked it behind him. Those gates were 8 feet tall and had stood for almost a century. Check. He speed-walked over to the side gate leading to his office, and locked it, too. Check. Shaking with nerves and the need for haste, he stitched that first layer of protection around himself. Janet had long said his house was nicely secluded, and that safety would work both directions.

Next, he burst into the house and went directly for the measuring tape. Rusty and cantankerous, the tape was hard to extend, and he snapped his fingers several times stretching the yellow strip across the length of his front yard. Getting even a rough estimate of 35 feet took far too long for Verbenk, who kept glancing over his shoulder at the street, at the other houses, at the very universe.

Then slam, slam, slam. He closed every window, every door, and locked those that would. Check. Next, he searched room to room for a roll of painter's tape or duct or what-the-fuck-ever tape. Finally hitting the jackpot, he found an old, linty roll of the masking variety.

He looked at the time. *Shit. Hurry, man.*

Verbenk started to measure. He stretched the tape from the front door through the foyer—only 18 more feet—and then down the hallway and past the formal dining room, before he set down a boundary with a piece of tape. Noting, for the second time that day, that 100 feet is indeed a big, big space.

He taped and taped against the ticking clock. How quickly would she abandon the lake? How quickly would another car arrive for her? Missing no radius of exposure, he measured the garage on the west side of the house. He measured his office. In terms of the backyard, there was easily 75 feet, followed by the protected ravine and wetland, which gave him plenty of safety.

Within 15 minutes, Verbenk had measured himself into a corner. Or rather, after taking account of Janet's 100-foot radius, he'd taped himself into one room. Or not even. He was in the kitchen, which had an eating nook and an attached TV area—though the kitchen's pantry was half in and half out of safety. Also out of bounds: his office; his bedroom upstairs; the stairs in general, both up and down—even if they lay merely in the Emotional Zone. He knew he would broadcast in any zone right now.

Just as the doctor leaned against the kitchen wall and began to slide down to the floor, the buzz of his intercom sounded. The sharp chime stabbed, and he froze, not even breathing. The intercom buzzed again.

Then, "You bastard," said Janet with volume-constrained rage across every room in his house.

He hyperventilated. She could be at either the front or side gates. He couldn't tell, but it didn't matter, because he was alone. Verbenk reassured himself of this point again and again. You're alone. You're finally alone. (You'll always be alone.)

"My wallet was in that bag," she seethed. "My driver's license and credit cards are at the bottom of the lake. The binoculars, of course, plus my key fob! Do you know how much BMW charges for those?!" For a moment, her finger must have still been pressing the transmit button, because he could hear the background noise of the outside world.

He could hear her rattle his locked gate. Then a cut back to silence.

For the space of 10 Mississippis, he waited. Then another buzz, this time from the other gate, he was sure. She was already systematically testing his hasty siege defenses. The silly woman didn't know this was for her own good. Making her ill with his crisis would be a self-flagellating blow too far.

"I know you're in there," said Janet, followed by a long mashing of the buzzer, sending that annoying sound from his ear drums into his skull, vibrating his brains.

But she didn't know he was in here, Verbenk soothed himself. Not for sure. Via common sense, sure, but not telepathically, at least. The telepath was caged outside, surely tilting her head off its axis, but hearing... nothing.

Oh, the bliss of nothing. Of being nowhere. That's what he needed right now, and he'd defend that nothing at all costs.

Buzzer still ringing in one constant, urgent screech, he didn't have the energy to stand. Instead, Verbenk scuttled farther into the kitchen on hands and knees, and pressed his back into the wall of the island, his scrawny legs spread and his normally ignorable belly spilling out in between.

A moment of cut silence, which made him freeze in place, then, "What were you thinking?" she asked, seething. "I have no idea what you're playing at, but this doctor-patient, therapeutic whatever-it-is is now over. You hear me? Fucking over."

An appliance whirred to life from surprisingly close by, and Verbenk turned, realizing that the wine fridge was still within the safe zone. *Thank you, Jesus*, he sent heavenward. He crawled toward the mini fridge and retrieved a half-full bottle of wine. He pried the cork out with his teeth and spat, was pleased when it hit the glass patio door to the backyard with a satisfying bong.

But she wasn't done, coming back louder now and less cautious. "You're insane. You know that. *You* are the insane one."

He nodded to no one in agreement about his own ineptitude, held the bottle up to toast it, then took a big, long pull, swallowing so hard he almost cramped his tongue.

"Now, I'm sure you remember since you have such *recent* experience," said Janet, her voice echo-warped down the tile hallway in between him and the speaker. He could picture it: one fist on her hip, eyes squinting with purpose. "But I'd like to remind you of your duties of doctor-patient confidentiality. If I hear one word about myself... or the health of my uterus... in the press or from anyone at all... I'll know who talked, because only family knows."

Of course. She worried more about the infertility than the telepathy in the end. If only she'd told him—though perhaps that open door would have just given him more space to fuck up.

"Plus, yeah, plus, I have dirt on you," she continued. "You can't tell anyone shit."

Pulling again at the wine, he accepted that truth, too. *You're all truth today, Janet. You won*, he broadcast, though he knew himself out of range. The process felt so common to him now that he failed to care. *Go away. You'll be fine without me, right? You're fine. Just perfect.*

"OK," she said, holding the button, taking the time to choose her words. "I guess that's it. That's that. Now... goodbye," she said, and silence descended on his hastily-built haven. His haven of— taking another look around— one and half rooms of privacy, plus a powder room. His frenzy spent on nest-building, he slumped farther onto the floor.

This was it. That was that.

The malpracticing doctor—so mal, his license should have been seized, and maybe he should forfeit it himself now—had been running on nothing but ego and perhaps a bit of the Dunning–Kruger effect, which said that the stupid are too stupid to understand how stupid they are. For decades, he'd been walking around with a superior attitude and little else of importance other than the names of important-sounding concepts like the Dunning–Kruger effect. But no more.

So this was what falling felt like. This was the smell of rotting meat. The last spark of his redemptive hope fizzled to wet ash under the wine, and there was something freeing in that. The freedom to give the fuck up for real, like he'd wanted to for... years, he supposed. Definitely for the last few months.

And this utter, frantic surrender wasn't just about Janet and his failure with her, but with the life plan itself. Sherman had been so adamant about young Verbenk's life plan, as if it would zip him up against failure. The right schools, the right profession, the supposedly right symbols of success and normalcy. Sherman, who loved to say this is right and wrong, true and false; chaos and order, us and them.

How disappointed he'd be now. Or perhaps he'd long ago guessed this would be the outcome. Verbenk was now a person too low for his own standards. A quarantine was what this masking-tape house was, keeping his horror from infecting the rest of the world. Yes, and a quarantine was in order, for everyone's good. Pulling his life into such a small diameter felt like the closest thing to erasing himself and his stains from the history and future of the world.

Therefore, he actually wasn't hiding like a coward, was he? He was sacrificing himself for the greater good, and so Verbenk nobly slurped his medicine, stumbled over to his couch and crawled up on it as if to die.

*D*erek Verbenk, regressed to the maturity of age 11, didn't shower for two days. On the third, he took his chances and snuck upstairs at 3:30 a.m. for a quick rinse—which was interrupted by a sudden noise and therefore remained unfinished, his hair greasy. Then there were four days more. Or five? Several times in the middle of the night, out of necessity, he'd chanced the stairs down to the basement, where he unearthed several boxes of expensive French wine and a case of Sherman's favorite scotch. Verbenk didn't usually like scotch, but he found likes and dislikes were for people who deserved them.

He'd fired the maid rather than explain himself, ditto the gardener. He canceled every appointment of his non-thriving home practice. He didn't shave. Didn't clip his nails. Didn't give a flying fuck about anything, even the almost constant body aches caused by sitting/lounging/eating/sleeping on the couch in the living room, which faced the giant TV. Strangely, comically, the "Popular on Netflix" category had suggested *Buffy the Vampire Slayer*, and he'd fallen into that universe scotch-soaked and head first.

Initially, he watched the teenager crap because he knew Sherman would not have approved. Then he continued because it had so many nice, time-killing seasons to next-episode through. And eventually, the fake blood and violence was distraction from the real kind that took place in that mental hospital, where he shouldn't have left her. He should never have left his mom alone.

He'd always been her keeper. Also her clown. He remembered pulling faces through the backseat window as she pumped gas outside in order to make her smile. He remembered magneting drawings and highly graded papers to the fridge for her. He remembered buying milk and bread on the way home from first grade, and her teaching him to make grilled peanut-butter-and-honey sandwiches. Tears wet his cheeks and snotted up his upper lip and would have flooded his whole life, if he let them.

Vampires were more immediate and stomped sandwiches underfoot. The *Buffy* universe in fact made more sense than this one with its measurable units, predictable patterns, campy comfort and enough action to keep his eyes mostly open so they didn't close on images of his mom. He'd already dreamt of the urn, which he'd held between funeral and reception in the back of the car. So light, floating away, and his dream fingers were fat and slippery with sweat.

Over that time, the intercom had sounded a dozen times—just buzzes, short and long, sometimes in patterns —and his cell rang and rang. But those were messages from another world, or so it felt. Once, right after a dawn before which he hadn't slept, Janet buzzed, waited, and spoke for the first time.

"You're a selfish, selfish man, Verbenk," she'd said, and he'd crunched his knees closer to his chest on the couch where he lay. He'd literally put the blanket over his head, creating a funk of his own breath beneath. "Are you going to just stay in there forever?"

Janet buzzed out a shave-and-a-haircut rhythm, then added, "Fine, be that way, but I thought you should know, everyone's trash bins blew over in the wind last night and your yard is full of garbage and leaves."

Her texts over that time, on the other hand, were more verbal and arrived in pairs or triplets.

Janet: *U there?*

Janet: *Where else would u be, though, right? You said I couldn't hide in my house, but now you are? Hypocrite much?*

Janet: *You owe me $126 and eight hours of time on the phone and at the DMV. Write a check. You know where I live.*

Janet: *What's that? Me? Oh, I'm doing great, thanks for asking. I've decided to take up yoga. It's all good!* 👍👍👍

Janet: *Never mind. The teacher deals oxy out of the locker room. I'd tell you the whole story but you'd enjoy it too much.*

Janet: *Orin's leaving for D.C. in a few days, and we're still dead in the water. It's hell being around him right now. I don't know what to do. Who to talk to. Nowhere to go.*

Janet: *Not that you care.*

Janet: *What was it you thought? Idle hands get manicures?*

Janet: 👍

The day he received that last text, mid-morning, he was scrolling through the entire history again, shaking his head, when the intercom buzzed.

Verbenk looked at the nearest masking-tape border, by the pantry and the hallway to the foyer. It was curling slightly off the tile, but was still there; he was still safe. He was standing in front of the open fridge in only his boxer shorts, a piece of stale, deli-sliced Swiss cheese halfway to his mouth, and he suddenly felt the open air around his naked legs, but he reminded himself: The contagion is contained.

"Hello?" Janet called through the empty rooms. "I know you're in there. This is important. I need to talk to you."

Like a defiant mouse, Verbenk nibbled at his cheese, grabbed a sports drink, closed the door of the fridge and waited.

"Be aware," Janet said all sober determination. "I'm coming in. There's something I can only talk about with you."

Verbenk's furry, ill-groomed eyebrows furrowed. Him? She knew who he was now. She should know better. His stomach filled with cold dread. What had he done now? In a thoughtless flurry, for a moment he began to collect the bottles and cans and burrito wrappers on the counter into the recycle bin, which clanked embarrassingly and quickly ran out of room.

Then he stopped, because it's not like he actually had a guest coming over. There was nothing she could do. The imposing gates, the ample yards. If she broke into the garage, he'd call the cops. That's right. He'd call the cops.

He looked down at his naked legs. Maybe.

Not knowing what else to do, Verbenk began making coffee—instant stuff, Orin would be horrified—and as it brewed, he rubbed his forehead and waited. He stared out the sliding glass door and wall of windows to the back-yard, the glass more than just a barrier to him. He was no longer part of the world beyond that glass. It all went on without him.

There was enough in the coffee carafe for one cup, so he grabbed it, letting a few drops fall from the machine onto the exposed hot burner. He was pouring the liquid into a mug and thinking about adding Irish cream—there might be some far back in the freezer—when he froze.

In his peripheral vision, something moved in the yard. Turning slowly, as if through honey, Verbenk watched a jeaned leg swing over the top of the privacy fence. The coffee machine dripped and sizzled, dripped and sizzled, and then Janet was sitting upright atop the stone wall on the other side of the pool, her face visible. Her hair was caged in a severe-intentioned bun, though tendrils flew wild about her face, and her eyes were shadowed and sad.

He was still holding the carafe in one hand, the half-full mug in the other. Their gazes met across the 75 feet between them, close enough that he knew she could feel his emotions, because whoa, doggie, he went from numb to maximum emotions in two seconds flat. He felt like an under-rock creature exposed to bright light. Tears he wouldn't have been able to explain poured over his cheeks as he stood there, otherwise still as a statue.

Assault from the rear. He hadn't planned his siege defense adequately.

Janet swung another leg over, carefully slid down the wall to stand in his grass in her sporty little jacket, then immediately began to stride around the pool and toward him with confidence, but with her hands raised. Showing she was unarmed. But a telepath was always armed.

"Don't do it," he said, forcing a calm authority he was good at projecting, but no longer believed. "I will call the cops."

That threat did stop her momentarily, one foot hanging in mid-step. Then she shook her head and held up her hands to frame her lips, which dramatically mouthed: Do it, then.

Shit. She could hear him clearly now and knew he'd do no such thing. Verbenk's mental barrier was officially breached.

Throwing the carafe and mug onto the counter, "I'm sorry!" he screamed into the kitchen-living room. Then he turned tail and bolted into the front half of the house, leaving the television blaring, tile slapping under his bare feet. He knew he was being ridiculous, but the amorphous, pressing fear was unstoppable. Past doorways and art niches, he instinctively headed for the front door. Grasping tight its bronze handle, he stopped and did not turn it, because he was undressed. Because his phone was still on the kitchen counter and the outside world was frightening, and really, because he had nowhere else to go but here.

In the kitchen, the almost melodic ringing of a knuckle on glass. Bong, bong, bong.

"Come back, Verbenk, please." Janet's glass-muffled voice carried through the hallway to his ears, though she must have been almost shouting to be heard. "Please, come here."

He pressed his hands against his ears, not so much to silence her as to bookend his brain and get his clouded thoughts in order. He knew she was too close, too close. Hand to his chest, clutching his plain white T—was it the same one he'd been wearing under his polo at the park?—he tried to formulate a plan, but no plans came. Even the comfort of plans had deserted him.

Bong, bong, bong, she tapped on the glass. "Come here. I'm not going to hurt you. And I don't care what you look like."

His eyes squinted open. Giving up on staying out of range—the house alone simply wasn't big enough—he took several steps toward the hallway to the kitchen and peeked around the corner. Verbenk finally got a view of his patient behind glass in the kitchen—though who was the caged animal, the exhibit, and who was the gawker, he wasn't sure. Her cheeks were pink with exertion. So petite in the flesh, smaller than he remembered, though it had been only a week. She was so very human.

Their eyes locked. Janet showed him her palms. Was she trembling? No, couldn't be. Janet was made of steel. Janet was competent and powerful—and loved—and not the type to tremble. And oh, there it was. His leftover anger and the pain of her public betrayal, screaming his secrets into the world.

So, "You're trespassing!" he shouted down the hall, through the glass, recalling the things she'd called him. Broken and disgusting and incompetent.

"I know, and I'm sorry," came the muffled reply. The wind ruffled stray tendrils of hair and rocked her body, and for a moment, she was focusing somewhere not him—somewhere in the middle distance, deep in thought or perhaps overwhelmed in handling his mind. She then shook herself back aware and wiped her eye, sniffing.

"Why are you here?" Verbenk crossed his arms and emerged from hiding, taking a few steps toward the kitchen until only a dozen feet lay between them. If she wanted to feel him, to put her tentacles into his brain, he'd show her the extent of it. She could see the whole sideshow if she wanted. His voice breaking, he asked, "What is so goddamn important that you can't just leave me alone? I'm doing no one any harm."

Except himself, and he didn't count. Now that she'd experienced the full tempest of his true self, surely she'd realize that and retreat. He wasn't worth it.

"I'm sorry," she repeated with not even a flare of reciprocal anger. Scarily earnest. "Sorry to be here. To have been so mean. I am invading, I see that now, and it seemed very important at the time, five minutes ago, that I talk to you, but now..."

She leaned her forehead against the glass momentarily, seeming dazed and frightened, and her ragged expression finally made Verbenk curious. And worried.

"What?" he asked, reaching his hand out as he closed the space between them, striding right up to the glass, her mirror on the other side.

Straightening, her hands in her jacket pockets, she breathed in deep, fueling up, her chest expanding with the effort like a thin balloon.

"But forget about me and what I came for. Back there?" said Janet, gesturing toward the open space. She must have crossed the low fence bordering the area a block away and walked the muddy extent along the ravine, and sure enough, her shoes were a mess. "On my way, I passed Christine's house. Close enough to hear, and I heard Christine."

A bolt of fear and shame struck Verbenk down to another level of self-hatred. Christine! The name of his patient finally fully cleared his head, far more than the awful coffee ever could have. He hadn't even considered her in days. She was in sunny, enviable Europe.

"No, she's not, and she doesn't want to live anymore, doc," said Janet, holding up one of her bare wrists to show him. Pale, slender. "And she knows which direction to cut."

6

"**S**he never said," said a frantic Verbenk, standing half in and half out of the laundry room as he dug in a basket of clothes, still clean but far from dryer-fresh. "I saw no indications of..." He shook his head. "So what did...? How did...?"

As Janet made hurrying motions with her hands, agitating the air, he stripped off the old T, chose the first shirt to hand and slung it on. He pressed its wrinkles against the body heat of his belly to no avail, but it didn't matter. Time—which had felt swampy for him lately, minutes like mire on his feet—seemed to be lurching back into existence, once again of essence to something.

One of his patients was suicidal.

"When?" Verbenk asked, finally stumbling into the most essential information. "When did you hear this?"

"Pants," said Janet, pointing the doctor back toward the basket. In the pile, half buried by tube socks, he found a pair of old khakis made into embarrassing cut-offs for around-the-house shorts. But there was no other option. Verbenk slung them on, closed the button at the waist— unaccustomed to the bind of non-elastic after several days of slobbery—and repeated, "When? Had she— Had she already—?" He seemed incapable of completing a question, his tongue unable to keep up with his thoughts.

"No. No? No. At least, not as of ten minutes ago." Janet hustled him toward the front of the house as if herding chickens, with shooing sweeps of her hand, which only increased Verbenk's nervous momentum. "I wasn't ex- pecting... I was only coming round that way to see if I could reach *you* from that direction, but—"

He snapped, "Your plan was to climb my fence to better yell at me?"

"No. I wanted to hear you say sorry," she said, and they traded accusatory looks before she went on, "But what I came for doesn't matter as much as what I heard."

"What did you hear? Be specific," demanded Verbenk as he dug in the cave under the coats in the closet for a pair of sneakers. Which he last seen about a decade ago, but all he found were dress shoes and snow boots and fallen cashmere scarves. He emerged back into the light with an older set of loafers, replete with tassels, and he hesitated.

"Just put them on, you fool," said Janet, flicking the back of her hand against his shoulder. "There are more important things at stake than your outfit at the moment.

It was a nuclear cloud of... numb despair, if that makes sense. Urgent, numb despair. And jumbled images. What looked like a towel, a small hand towel stained red, and *thoughts* of blood, the relief of blood." Her voice was high and trembling with overwhelm. "And like I said out there, that people who mean it go up and down."

She cringed and raised her hands to her head at the mere memory. Her nose was pink, her cheeks damp and her breath pure hyperventilation. Verbenk wasn't faring much better.

"Was this ideation or action you overheard?" he clipped as he put on the shoes. If Christine had acted on what Janet overheard, they were operating within a few literal heartbeats. When Janet failed to answer, he stood and grabbed her by the shoulders, repeating, "Only ideation?"

She was shaky legged in fear, blinking. "I think so. No. I'm 100 percent sure she's not done it. That would have felt even more..." Swallowing now as if nauseated, Janet teetered on her feet. "It would have been different. This felt like preparation. Cleaning things? Freshening sheets on all the beds. An empty walk-in-closet."

A chill suffused Verbenk's torso. Tidying up after herself. Tying loose ends, putting affairs in order. A textbook warning sign of suicide. He pressed his lips together ineffectually.

Janet said, "And there were blades." Her voice began to peter out to a whisper. "A bouquet of blades."

'I sometimes wish they would have just cut it off,' Christine had said about her pretty, little, surgery-enhanced

nose. Self-harm or thoughts of self-destruction were other checks on the Suicide Watch list. *'If I was ugly,'* she'd said, *'I'd be allowed to be unhappy.'*

Stupid. Stupid, stupid, stupid. He was a literal idiot. All the signs had been there, but separately, like unconnected dots, and his mind had been directed toward another puzzle—and too much toward himself.

He snapped back to focus when Janet slumped between his hands, her eyes unfocused. She was taking in too much emotion. First suicidal absorption, then a good layer of Verbenk's own panic on top. His panic never did her any good.

"OK, OK. It's OK. Let's take a breath then, for everyone's sake." Verbenk inhaled for both of them, nostrils flaring. He caught sight of himself in the foyer's antique gold-framed mirror. Gray-skinned and unshaven and looking like a suburban dad about to hungover mow the lawn, but he let his appearance not matter, even if it did. All that mattered now was life.

Fighting his natural instincts, he tried to clear his mind as he'd done so many times in his office and to create a bubble of calm. Immediately Janet's shoulders relaxed between his hands and he released her to lean upon the post of the foyer's stairway.

"I wasn't listening," he said. "To Christine."

"No, no, no. Oh, it wasn't just you," said Janet, more steadily standing now. "I feel awful because I knew, too, but I also didn't, you know?" She began to pace a few steps one direction and the other. Her shoes no longer so muddy, most of it now in a footprint trail across his kitchen. "Until today, until that blast up close, I wasn't sure what I was hearing—feeling—from her. I mean, I did know she was feeding you a line of bullshit about going on vacation, but—"

"What?! When? Wait..." The cogs in Verbenk's brain began to move again, creaking in complaint. "When she came to the door during your drop-by session that morning," he answered his own question, pointing his index finger at Janet. "When she said she was—"

"Oh, she was never going to Europe. She was never going anywhere except right there," said Janet, poking her finger in the general direction of Christine's house, four doors down. "Apparently her husband *is* overseas all this month, but her getaway was being home by herself. And something about an art project."

"And you didn't tell me?" Verbenk closed the distance between them, thrusting his chest and chin at the smaller woman. She thrusted hers back and they stood, toe to toe on the shiny, white tiles of his impressive, never-used foyer.

"Is it my job to spill every secret?" she shouted. "Besides, I rather figured that if *she* didn't trust you with the truth, why should I?"

Deflating his chest, deflating his ego, Verbenk would have sunk into the earth then and there were it possible. "Fair enough."

"I hear so many things," she said quietly, hiding her face in her hands.

"Oh, never mind, never mind," he said, to both of them. They were where they were, and it didn't matter how they got there just now. "None of this is your fault."

Wiping an index finger under each eye, she sniffed again as if to put the sniffles away for good. "There's no time for fault. Now, come on."

She strode to the front door and opened it. Without warning, the poor door, so used to being closed, swung open upon a pile of scuttling dry leaves on his front steps. Verbenk hesitated, fear hijacking his system. Fear and doubt and self-hatred. The crisp air stirred against his bare legs, and his glasses revealed themselves fogged with smudges in the afternoon sun.

"Wait," he said, standing upon the threshold while Janet loomed behind him, ready to shoo him on. "If she's been intentionally hiding such pain, if she doesn't trust me to that extremity, how exactly am I supposed to intervene?"

Janet turned back to shrug and tugged down her zip-up fitness jacket. "I know. She doesn't exactly like me, either."

"Then what the fuck are we going to do?" he asked, cleaning the lenses on his disheveled T-shirt and shivering in the great outside. Outside, where everyone could see him. He breathed. In and out. The air was fuel.

"Best I can figure, we're going to do what we practiced. What we trained for," Janet said, shaking her big-screened, well-thumbed phone to get his attention then turning to jog down the walk. "You coming?"

Verbenk's mouth quirked in a fatalistic smile. Of course he was coming.

*T*he Blum's house was typical for the neighborhood: respectably old but kept rigorously new. Rather than Victorian like his, theirs was built in the 1920s, Spanish inspiration, two stories plus a taller decorative turret circled by windows. The walls were covered in artisan-spread, earth-toned stucco, and the house's tulip-shaped balconies of wrought iron protruded like cages. Wrought iron for the lighting sconces bracketing the three garage doors.

More iron crisscrossed the glass pane in the front door, which was oversized, at least 9 feet tall. The door loomed at Verbenk as he and Janet approached along the sidewalk, her walking ahead, glancing back every third step as if to make sure he hadn't escaped—and her limbs seeming to get heavier and tighter as they approached. Twice she held the back of her hand to her mouth, as if in nausea.

The doctor's loafers squeaked to a halt at the head of the Blum's walk. Despite what seemed like a ticking time bomb on his hands, his hurry boiled away into dread. Going to cold knock on the door of a woman engaged in a secret plan to...

"At least you didn't find her," Sherman had said. In fact, such was one of the few things he'd said to Verbenk directly afterward, during the official transition of custody, as his uncle so formally called it. There had been child protective services and paperwork and generic governmental rooms where he was interviewed or made to wait. "And you couldn't have stopped it. She was determined to succeed."

He'd heard whispers sitting in those beige rooms. How she'd packed up all her belongings first, the most considerate suicide anyone at the hospital had ever met. Even made her bed, was the rumor. She left everything but that mirror from her purse, from the beach—

Again Janet flicked her hand against Verbenk's upper chest, and he realized that today was the first time the woman had deigned to touch him, though again she drew immediately back.

"Don't dwell there right now," she said, and her forehead was creased, obviously absorbing pain. "This time is not like that time."

One quick, dark laugh. "It's not?" he asked. Sure seemed like history repeating itself to him. Two different women, both so ready to voluntarily self-destruct.

"No, it's not. Now *I'm* here." Janet pointed toward her temple and forced her voice upbeat. "And I'll be there with you. Well..." Looking left and right behind her, she qualified, "Well, I'll be out *here*, but after she lets you in, I'll sneak up, hide in the bushes and be with you."

Phone still in hand, she waved vaguely toward the house's front bay window, which were sure enough fronted by hearty bushes bristling with autumn-colored berries, and urged him, "You know you have to do this."

Verbenk was skeptical. Verbenk was scared shitless. Pale as a sheet and Lamaze breathing, so was Janet. He could see their old friend, the vein on her neck. Her hand snapped to cover it. She was so focused, obviously struggling to contain what she was overhearing, but keeping control. Not running away.

"Yes, I have to do this, but why are you?" he asked, the question formed and asked in the same split second—and perhaps he was stalling. "After everything you said about people at the park. Why get involved with Christine?"

Without hesitation, "Because Christine has a son." Janet pressed her lips together and glanced at the Blum's door. "I've felt the pain of a son for his mother's suicide. No one should have to bear that. Ever," she said, and Verbenk felt a warm and unexpected stab through his ribcage, trembling his heart. "Now, go! I'll text!" she promised. "Go!"

Hissing the last word, she jogged away to the edge of the Blum's yard, where a hedge of more bushes would obscure her from the front door's view.

Swallowing away the taste of bile in his mouth, the doctor forced his feet up the path, plodding as if against gravity. The porch he approached seemed abandoned. Drifts of leaves had gathered against the front door, where at least a week's worth of daily papers was also languishing. His middle-aged heart fluttered in his chest as he approached, but his arm did not raise toward the doorbell. His arm felt glued to his side.

I might as well not get up in the morning, and no one would notice, she'd said. *I might as well be talking to myself.*

He prodded his forehead several times with his index finger, as if to force himself to stay in reality—with vision clear of his own funk and fog—then he pressed the door-bell before he could grow second thoughts. Instead, it was his memories that grew as he waited.

No, he hadn't found her body. That honor belonged to the orderlies who searched the janitor's closet once she was noticed missing, where he was told she'd barred the door, sliced her wrists and bled carefully into the janitor's mop bucket. The mirror case and all but one shard of its broken glass pre-placed in a nearby dustpan.

Leaving a mess would have been discourteous, after all. But this time was not last time?

Still, the door remained shut and silent. He fidgeted, feeling he'd explode if he didn't. He really couldn't make himself stand here much longer. His phone buzzed in his pocket.

Janet: *She's there. Ring again. Make it awkward enough & she'll let you in.*

He obeyed, hearing the chimes ring out for a second time into the house, which was giving a very good impression of being empty. A breeze rustled the leaves and brought up goosebumps on his inexplicably sweaty neck, holding with it a taste of Halloween, a taste of rot and iron (or blood) and death and funerals and loss.

Verbenk had never seen his mom's body and no photos of it existed, but his grief had been yanked from its repression and he could see the scene in his mind anyway, as vibrant and stylized as comic art. Then he saw the same pen-and-ink drawing morph to have Christine's face, an artist painting in the red pool of blood on the tiles beneath her cheek.

And such was the place he emerged from when the Blum's door opened, first a crack and then a shoulder-wide gap—Christine's slender shoulders, slender neck, pale face—and so he was primed and ready to assume the worst when he saw red stains upon the woman's white shirt.

Nooo, he yelled to Janet.

"Are you OK?!" Verbenk practically shouted, his clumsy fingers reaching toward her hands, her wrists, hoping to apply blood-staunching pressure immediately.

"Dr. Verbenk!" Christine took a step back into the house, narrowing the door, but he could still see a whole slice of her body head-to-toe. Her body, standing on strong and steady legs, obviously—thankfully—still well-fed with blood and clad in jeans, which were cuffed several times at the ankle. She asked, "What are you, what do you—?"

Verbenk's eyes hopscotched over his patient, noting that her face was composed, if surprised. Not merely slender, her hands were downright skinny and showing their age, but were also clean and holding a rag that was covered with red stains. But not only red, it turned out. The towel was also spotted with grease and ink and smelled of solvent.

His eyes widened in understanding and hopeful doubt. A painter's rag. A painter's rag could easily appear in a quick mental image as a towel of blood, now couldn't it?

Now couldn't it, Janet? Telepathy was an inexact science, right?

Of course, Janet wasn't there to answer. The phone in Verbenk's hand remained silent, but he took some heart. Meanwhile Christine was still staring at him, open-mouthed.

Hand on his heart in apology, "I'm, I'm sorry," Verbenk stuttered, gesturing at the rag and also her spattered-red shirt. It was a smock of some sort, perhaps made out of a cast-off man's shirt, thin and baggy. "I thought it was..."

"Blood. Yes. Dave has mentioned that in the past, too. Sorry." Relaxing slightly, she tucked the paint-stained rag into the back pocket of her jeans and patted at her hair, but didn't further open the door. "I canceled my appointments, yes? Is everything OK with..."

Christine tilted her head in question, obviously unsure what to make of this visit. He watched her eyes run him up and down, taking in the odd attire, but he could think of nothing to say. *A worried neighbor who can read your mind through walls sent me to check on you?* Nope. He rocked forward and back on his feet, rubbing his neck, stalling.

"Yeah, so, you're probably wondering why I'm here," Verbenk finally settled on, hoping the lead in would give him time to think of an excuse. But no excuse came. He could see Christine's polite patience waning, and panic began to creep into his chest cavity, spreading like seeping concrete.

The phone clutched in his right hand buzzed.

Beaming out gratitude, Verbenk mouthed an apology to Christine for the impoliteness and took a quick glance at the screen. Once read, he thumbed a button to hide the message—*Janet: Say u know about pharmacy*—he then let his arm hang, hopefully casually, at his side.

"Sorry," he said to Christine tentatively, unsure how to use this cryptic message, "but you see, the, uh, pharmacy..."

Verbenk needn't have been worried about how he was to complete the sentence, because the last word struck her face almost physically, rippling over her defenses. *Bingo.* How thrilling, how Janet had handed him this secret passage into his patient's mind. A shortcut to the meat of the matter.

"We..." He fumbled, trying to improvise, but instead settling on the time-trusted stock expression: "We should talk about that, no?"

"Dammit," Christine answered. With a little stomp of her foot, she let go of the door and frame, and stepped backward into the foyer. The doctor read resignation, per-haps even defeat, upon her pretty features—but nothing of sadness—as she waved for him to enter, craning her neck behind him as he did so, as if to see if he was fol-lowed. "I was afraid of this."

Verbenk scuttled through the opening into the dark-ness of the house, feeling the interloper. The attacker now when he was so recently the besieged. He craned his neck to catch the last sliver of the outside as Christine shut the door, and his nervous heart swelled in relief: Knees bent, hunched like a cartoon burglar, Janet was scurrying across the lawn toward the house-hugging bushes.

Then the outside was gone, and it was just him. Just him and Christine and the elephant in the room.

"I'm assuming the pharmacy called you," Christine said, locking the deadbolt.

He blinked, his eyes to adjusting back to the dim indoors, but once they did, he chilled. The house's interior screamed "affairs in order." The open main level that pooled out from where he stood looked like a spread in a magazine. Leather couches with nail-head trim, a stone fireplace stretching floor to ceiling, travertine tiles on the floor along with several thick, wool area rugs. Aspirational but accessible.

To his right, an art niche in the wall. To his left, a mosaic-topped table with one bowl for keys and a larger one filled with decorative balls. The kind of useless, pretty shit designers like. But every decorative ball was dusted, every couch pillow in the adjacent room freshly plumped. The air carried the scent of Pine-Sol and the electric aftersmell of a vacuum.

Here there was no laundry left to crust in baskets, no nest of sweat-funky blankets on the couch like in his own den of depression. The only sign Verbenk could see that something might be emotionally amiss was the far wall—designed to be a wall of windows looking out on that lovely, ravine open space behind their houses, but was currently a wall of blinds of a rich neutral shade.

Christine cleared her throat softly, prettily, and tucked a stray hair behind her ear. Except for a slight breathless quality about her voice, Verbenk would have sworn this woman was not only OK, but perfect. Her smock shirt hung off her lean shoulders in an elegant line, the baggy pants somehow emphasizing the lithe limbs inside. A woman who could make a sack look stylish.

"About the pharmacy, honestly," she said, walking around him, forcing him to pivot to follow, until she stood as boundary between him and her home, "I would have easily just held off if I knew it was going to be a big thing."

He nodded, as if he and not Janet knew what this pharmacy business was actually about.

She continued, "I told the pharma tech not to worry about it, that she didn't need to call you or anything, but I guess…" Christine shrugged. "Really, it was no big deal."

"You wanted a refill," Verbenk realized and said aloud simultaneously. Quickly, he did the pill math. There was no way she needed more since his last script, even if she were abusing them, so what could have been her excuse other than, well, amassing a large, final dosage—of Xanax, which wasn't ideal, but which didn't stop many people from trying. When that didn't work, her mind had moved toward the blades Janet overheard. "You said you needed the meds because you were," he guessed, "going out of the country? A vacation refill?"

She colored. "Right." Meaty bullseye.

"But you're not out of the country," said the doctor, gently pointing toward her, her presence his Exhibit A. He realized his voice was one notch too loud, as if he was projecting for Janet's benefit, which was fucking ridiculous, so he turned it down.

"Right. Um, change of plans," she said, adjusting the collar of her shirt with a downward tug. "Doug went without me, and I decided to use the opportunity for a personal vacation, but at home. A— what do they call it these days?"

His lip curled in distaste. "A *stay*-cation."

"Such a horrible word," agreed Christine with thin laughter. "Again, my apologies for the inconvenience. I'll call in the next few days about setting up a new appointment."

She then propped a hand on her hip, a photogenic pose of effortless cool. She was dismissing him. She was *lying to him*—and so, so well. He was standing two feet in front of the woman, yet they were two people in separate shells.

What was he supposed to say now? *OK, but I'm really concerned that your house is too clean?* Right.

Instead, Verbenk offered, "Well, I suppose that... I, uh...wanted to..." He wiped his forehead. Unless something brilliant came to mind, he'd soon run out of nonsense to sputter.

His phone buzzed twice in quick succession. He seized on the distraction as a means of stalling, saying, "Excuse me one moment," and half turning his body to look at his text messages.

Janet: *Where's the dog?*

Janet: *Then ask her for coffee like a neighbor. She's too polite to say no.*

Smiling, acting, "I apologize for that," he said, turning back with a smile. "I always need to check in case it's a patient—" He shook the phone in explanation, pleased with his impromptu excuse. "—but forgive me. Hey, don't you have a sweet little dog?" Verbenk made a show of looking around the corners of the hallway and great room.

Her eyebrows furrowed. "Little? An Irish Wolfhound?"

Smoothing right over that glaring error, "Right," he said. "Where is the big guy?"

Christine's smile went brittle. "Georgia. *She's* with my son. We were going to be in Europe, and Eric loves long visits from her. I didn't want to take that away from him because I decided to... well."

Rehoming a beloved animal was certainly a form of giving away one's possessions—another warning sign! Oh, there was absolutely no mistake.

Verbenk marveled, because no one would guess. It was completely possible that nary a soul had any idea that this enviable human being no longer wanted to be one. He examined Christine's face. The former model had an ideal profile and no bad camera angle, but perhaps she should have pursued acting instead.

"Right," he said, then cleared his throat, ready now to follow all of Janet's advice to the letter. "But all this pharmacy stuff aside, I'm actually here for a favor. You see, I'm, um, fresh out of coffee and desperate. I'm wondering if you could maybe... spare a few beans? Or, is that the delicious aroma of coffee just now? Maybe I can just steal a cup?"

Sniffing hopefully, he blinked innocence, leaning hard on Christine's apparent weakness for social niceties.

He prodded, "Just a little neighborly coffee for a poor caffeine beggar."

Twisting her lips in indecision, she admitted, "There is some from this morning. It's cold now, but…" She turned her head toward the gourmet kitchen visible across the great room, reticent. "Are you anti-Starbucks or something?"

"Or something." His nose wrinkled involuntarily. Verbenk could picture Janet's eye-roll reaction from here. "I'd so greatly appreciate it, though. It's been a day already. You know?"

Christine's mouth remained ajar on the word no for several moments, but he waited her out, trying to be in no hurry, instead examining for the first time the painting in the art niche on the wall. Quite lovely, an almost photographically detailed stream captured in mid flow, the sandy oblong rocks of the riverbed distorted through the lens of water. He made appreciative noises to stretch the silence.

Then finally, to his relief but not his surprise—*thank you, Janet*—Christine sighed and said, "Fine. I just wrapped up something, so I have five minutes, I guess. Five minutes."

"Bless you," he said, smiling foolishly.

Christine pointed a thumb behind her and Verbenk followed the spattered rag in her back pocket farther into the posh living room. While her back was turned, his phone buzzed.

Janet: *She doesn't want you to go into her art studio.*

Well, then. Where was this art studio? The last thing Christine wanted him to see was likely the most important, probably in some way related to the culmination of her plan. As they walked, the doctor began to scan from side to side, looking for doorways and hallways to possible studios, but as he approached the kitchen, his eyes caught instead on an oblong painting hanging to just to the right of the breakfast bar, which Christine proceeded to go around toward the kitchen appliances. He couldn't help but approach. Obviously in the same style of the piece in the entry—glossy and hyperrealistic—but this time, a mountain lake.

A buzz.

Janet: *It's hers. She's the artist.*

Verbenk's chin drew back in surprise as he looked at the painting again.

"This is yours? You made this?" he blurted, before remembering her words in one of their past sessions: I have been known to do some art. *Damn.* He'd assumed she'd meant lower-case arts, as in arts and crafts rather than anything related to The Arts, but this work was seriously upper case.

"How did you know that?" Christine paused with the machine's coffee carafe in one hand, her fully exposed wrist blessedly undamaged. Right now. "But yes. That's right," she added, putting a mug of the cold coffee into the microwave and pressing a button. "Our sessions. I mentioned. You remembered."

"Mm-hm," he hummed, feeling his cheeks flush but moving further into the kitchen. He shook his head at his deafness, at all the things he didn't hear. "You didn't say that you were a real artist."

"Oh, I'm not," she said, waving away his words. "I never even studied art in school. I recently picked up an unfinished piece after years away, but it's not like I could support myself on it or anything. It's not like anyone wants to buy it."

The latter sounded like her husband's words, the doctor thought. "You've had shows?" he asked.

"Decades ago," shrugged Christine. "Now it's a hobby."

"It's a gift," he answered with sincerity.

Christine blushed, obviously nervous, her movements self-conscious. Her meaty issues so close to the surface. Verbenk's senses were alight with her discomfort, all his energies focused on this woman who couldn't admit.

"You must be really desperate to want my leftover coffee," Christine said as the microwave hummed. "It must be some kind of day indeed."

"Pardon?" asked Verbenk.

Christine tilted her head. "You said you had a day."

"Ah, yes," he said, then caught her gaze cutting to her left, toward what looked like a sunroom or enclosed patio at the extreme back of the house, its glass-paned French doors ajar. The studio, he was sure, though he put a question mark on the thought in his mind for Janet, his absent guide. "A... patient situation I'm dealing with today," he suggested. "A doctor's never off duty, you know."

He craned his neck, now seeing that the back section of the studio was green-house paned from waist level up, the glass stretching up to form half the room's ceiling. Brilliant sunlight, pouring from the ceiling spotlighted a large, wooden easel. "You don't mind if I...?" he asked casually, pointing toward his intention, but didn't wait for an answer.

"Wait—" Christine began, but was interrupted by the ding of the microwave. "No! I mean, yes. I mind."

Feigning deafness, Verbenk began to walk toward the forbidden room, the dangerous room. In the glassed corner sat a desktop cluttered with plastic trays and half-closed boxes of art supplies, and next to it a utilitarian file cabinet studded with magnets. Papers and postcards were taped to the greenhouse glass, curling at the edges.

"Dr. Verbenk!" Christine called from behind him.

His phone again buzzed in his hand when he was halfway to his destination.

Janet: You're going too far away. I'm losing you.

He paused, glancing toward the front door—measuring the distance of her 75-foot radius of clarity—then back toward the studio, and wondering if he should retreat.

Janet: *No! Go! I'll come around ravine side now. Give me a minute.*

Oh, he was going. There would have been no stopping the doctor now, anyway, because as he approached, his eyes locked on a series of mason jars on her pencil- and brush- and paper-strewn desk. A jar of pipe cleaners, one of sponge brushes, and another of blades. At least five or six X-Acto knives with pen-like handles bristled in a glass tumbler, their heads shaped like malign, sharpened beaks. A vase of blades placed dangerously sharp-side up. A bouquet of blades.

"Dr. Verbenk?" Christine called again. "Please, that's private."

"Your other work is just so stunning! I can't wait to see more!" he shouted back as excuse and pressed further.

Warm-cheeked, he hustled into the room like an awkward, out-of-shape ninja. On instinct, he dumped the blades from their tumbler and gathered them by the handles into both hands, feeling like the world's strangest bride, but he had only his pants pockets on him. That hiding place might cause more bloody trouble than it would prevent. He cast around instead for a drawer, an envelope or a safe spot of any sort. But then his eyes fell on the main studio wall and he instantly forgot that mission, hooked and mesmerized by what he saw.

Water. The surface of a puddle, smooth and glassy, filled a painting that was easily eight feet wide and five tall. A puddle of inestimable depth, the paint so smooth the water—disturbed by overlapping ripples—looked printed into the fabric of the canvas. Water imagery pervaded her work, he noted, though that detail was perhaps not the most striking. What shocked the most was the color of the water: red. Shades of red on red. Red rain plunking red ripples into red puddles of... maybe not water.

Blood? Of course. Janet had seen this, too.

A plastic drop cloth on the floor rustled under his feet as Verbenk stepped toward the painting, moving around a folding chair set up front and center to the canvas, the ample glass bathing the seat in sun. Still holding his grizzly bouquet, he looked out through the sunroom panes to the backyard and the close proximity of the back fence, and he realized: This is where Christine had been standing when Janet overheard.

At the moment, though, Janet was nowhere to be seen, even when he stood tiptoe to try to peek over the fence. She was absent when he needed her most, because this was as far as they'd planned: getting in to Christine. There hadn't been time for the more vital plan of how to get through to the woman, and now he was stuck alone, mid-caper, with no exit plan, holding a bouquet of death.

"Doctor?" asked Christine from just outside the room, startling him back to life. He quickly dumped the blades onto the top of the tall file cabinet, their fall thankfully muffled by paper.

Just then Christine appeared, holding a mug of coffee and nervously examining the room around him. Seeing if he'd disturbed anything, he suspected, and seeming relieved that her viewing for one was still as she'd set it, thankfully not noticing the blades' absence.

Her feet crunching across the drop cloth to get to Verbenk, "Here," she said bluntly, shoving the cup at him. Now so close together, he could match up the shades of paint splotches on her smock to the dozens of shades of red in the work. He could also now see the anger blooming beneath her mask of civility, saw that he was on thin fucking ice here, on the verge of being tossed out on his ear, and he was not going to lose someone else this way. Not again.

Still striving for casualness, smiling, he reached for the mug. Took a sip to stall for time. Guatemalan beans, he could have sworn. Everything connected today. Today, everything was on the line, but placed so on the spot, Verbenk's entire psychiatric education abandoned him. All that book learning, all those theories and techniques named after famous dead people, the case studies—all his scientific surety—seemed to have been drained from his brain and what was left in its place was just a hollow, fallible man.

"So, trouble with a patient?" asked Christine, gesturing at the phone still clutched in Verbenk's right hand. "I'm sorry about that, truly, but maybe you should—"

"Right." He, too, looked at the un-vibrating device, reminded of his excuses. "Um, yes. And I, well, obviously, I can't discuss the details with patient confidentiality and all," he continued, steamrolling over her coming invitation to get the fuck out of her house. "Obviously, but…"

But what? Think, man, think.

Janet? he called out, feeling adrift and alone and light-headed and paper-thin. Now that frenzy has stopped being his animating force, his own despair and uselessness and aching tired poured back in.

"But?" Christine prompted him, but then the phone buzzed, and Verbenk seized on its distraction and possible answers.

Janet: *Minor delay. omw. Try honesty. You're alike in angst, remember.*

Honesty? Verbenk frowned. That was all Janet had for him? Right. Because transparency had worked so well with

Janet herself. Janet, who loathed him, who picked up his reeking thoughts with pinched fingers and pinched nose.

"Well, I'm sure your patient trouble will all work itself out," said Christine, her arms across her belly protectively. "When you're back in your own—"

Verbenk cleared his throat to interrupt. Janet had proven herself time and time again, he remembered, and besides: He had nothing to lose. He was out on limb, certainly, but fuck it, he decided as he slid the phone into his back pocket.

"I said patient trouble, but honestly...?" he started, trying on the concept. He'd never been good with vulnerability. "Honestly, the real problem is sometimes not the patient," he finally said, his tone more resigned to the disclosure than he expected. "The problem is that I haven't been a very good doctor recently."

"Oh?" Christine began to drift about the room, aimlessly tidying, but he could sense her ears perked in his direction. "I don't see how that's any of my concern,"

Verbenk ran his eyes over a rack of clean, drying brushes. The painting was done, she'd said, and the materials were put away. She was so very close to the edge that it frightened him into admitting, unprompted, "I haven't even been a very good person lately, I suppose. Haven't quite been... present. For anyone. You included, I'm afraid. Or truthful with anyone for that matter."

He watched Christine's bare, slender neck as, facing away, she pretended to line up the already-queued colored pencils on her desktop. When he didn't continue,

"Forgive me," she said, turning profile toward him, "but why are you telling me this?"

Setting down his coffee—his literal pretense—he shrugged off the rest of his pretenses, too, answering, "I'm telling you this so you understand that when I found out that a patient of mine was keeping secrets—hiding the extreme nature of their emotional distress—" Verbenk scratched his stubble with his fingertips and observed how Christine hitched momentarily, as if frozen for a frame. "—well, how can it be their fault? When I was lying, too."

She slowly revolved to face the doctor and leaned against her desk, perched on its corner, her ankles crossed. Her arms still guarded, always guarded. Skeptically, her face smooth as her painting, she said, "I suppose we all have secrets."

"And some of us secret talents," he said, gesturing back toward the painting. "This is the project you just finished, I assume?" When she nodded, he continued, asking, "So what's its secret?" and closely watched her response.

Blinking, confused, Christine picked at something on the desktop. "That's a very doctorly thing to ask. I thought you were just a neighbor today in search of coffee." A weak smile, then an attempted subject-change joke. "Should I go get my checkbook?"

Honesty. Try honesty.

"Hey, just a little neighborly conversation here, right? Back and forth, give and take. But if you don't want to take a turn, I'll go again. My former partners fired me," he said, letting that rock ripple as it would. He was really trusting Janet's judgment here, watching Christine with his peripheral vision to see her reaction.

And actually, it was less difficult telling the second person than the first.

"I deserved it," he added, nodding at the floor and only in that moment accepting that truth. He'd deserved it. "I'm coming to terms with that," he realized and said aloud simultaneously.

For a moment, the model/artist/brilliant actor said absolutely nothing. Then finally, she pressed her lips together, considering.

"Back and forth, huh?" she asked, and shifted her weight foot to foot, otherwise unmoved. "Well, the painting. It's actually an old piece—" She thrust her chin toward her bloody masterpiece. "—and had been sitting unfinished in storage for years, until Dave left for Europe. I could only finish it if he wasn't here."

"Oh?" he asked, stepping closer to and feigning deep interest in the painting. Letting the silence stretch, using it like a crowbar.

"Yeah, he hates it," Christine continued. "Dave says that life should be about surrounding oneself with beauty, not darkness. He hates all things morbid." An uncomfortable laugh, too sharp—like cracking thin ice?

Committed now, though, Verbenk took the risk and lobbed a follow-up question over the net. "So which are you?" he asked, head tilted. "Beautiful, or morbid?"

A sad, lopsided smile. "Neither?" she softly replied. "But also both."

His glance darted toward her and away, only to catch her own glance doing the same. They seemed to agree that the floor, the painting and her artist's detritus were all far more interesting than each other. They gave each other that small privacy. Whatever it took, he thought, if she agreed to play honesty ball.

"So why'd they fire you?" Christine suddenly asked.

Initially startled and embarrassed, Verbenk again intentionally pressed down his fear and overcame his pretenses, which seemed—strangely—to only get easier.

"I took advantage of someone only because I needed personal comfort," he admitted, taking his turn. "And I have so many apologies to make. Apologies I don't know how to make—not least because I'm not legally allowed to."

Christine's eyebrows flew up in curiosity, but he shook his head in response.

"Can you beat that?" he asked, before he turned from her and sat down in the folding chair, so they both regarded the painting from equal and parallel distance, as if the other wasn't present.

He heard her shift herself in the silence, but waited.

"Eric has my artistic eye," she said from behind him. Like a narrator, like the soundtrack to the strange, still movie frame of the painting. "He's a gifted photographer—if his mother does say so herself—but he's following his father's path instead. He decided to pursue his MBA next year. Dave says, 'You can't support a life on art.'" She put on a stentorian tone that reminded Verbenk of his uncle. "He says, 'One doesn't get into Harvard Business and just walk away.'"

She sniffed, then added, "Kind of like, 'One doesn't just walk away from a Fashion Week contract to go to art school.' I don't want Eric to have that regret."

Wincing, Verbenk again relived half-heard comments in their sessions. She'd told him this in a roundabout way, hadn't she? He allowed this new perspective to edit the story he'd created for himself about who this woman was. Oh, how he'd oversimplified—and how much he could relate. Disappointment, regret, self-doubt, self-sabotage: Such common human dramas were no less painful for being universal.

"For me," Verbenk said, putting on the Sherman voice himself, "it was 'Verbenks are men of science. Pull it together and don't be an embarrassment!' or 'Put down that comic book and join the real world, young man!'"

Turning his head, Verbenk saw Christine squint at him, like a woman of her age—of their shared age, really—caught without her glasses, holding him at arm's length to see if she'd misread. Then the corner of her mouth quirked upward.

"Comics?" she asked, pulling back, incredulous but playful. "I admit. I had you pegged wrong. You're full of surprises today."

He also smiled, gently. His hope rose—gently there, too—because she was beginning to relax into his presence. A bridge was finally being built between them. Better late than never, he supposed.

"Please," he said, gesturing to the empty space beside him for her to somehow join him in sitting. The one chair, floating in the room's center like this, was such an odd detail. Awkward in an otherwise perfectly put away space. All affairs in order, but drop cloth still down? Very odd. Still, he asked, "Is it possible to join me?"

"I suppose."

He watched Christine walk to the corner, where several more folding chairs rested against the wall. She peeled one away from its compatriots—and happened to glance at the top of the nearby file cabinet as she did so. Verbenk's fist clenched, his forehead furrowed, and he waited as she noticed the X-Actos on top.

She paused with the chair under her arm. Her ponytail drooped in resignation.

"So I'm the patient? I'm the patient trouble?" Christine asked the wall rather than him. "You... know. Somehow you know."

Verbenk closed his eyes momentarily, his molten, turbulent heart about to pour out through his eyes, because, yeah. He knew exactly. Though she couldn't see him, he nodded. "Yes, I know."

Still frozen, she began, "How...? The pharmacy?" and turned her shocked face toward him.

Just then, Verbenk's phone buzzed back to life, lighting him up like a defibrillator shock. He hesitated, not wanting to break the spell, but felt he needed the guidance.

Janet: *Yes. Keep being you. It's working.*

Shifting on the flimsy chair, Verbenk slipped the phone back into his pocket and opened himself up, put on his most non-threatening and understanding face. He held his hand to Christine and gestured her toward him, brushing away her fright and his. Breathing through the vulnerability and fear. Making it not matter.

She took a shaky step toward him, holding the chair.

"Not the pharmacy," he said as she tentatively unfolded the seat, creating a front-row audience of two for her completed masterpiece.

"Then how?" she demanded, heavily slumping down into the chair as if she weighed 120 tons rather than 120 pounds.

"Superpowers," Verbenk answered with sincerity. "I can read your mind." He wiggled his fingers comically at her. "There are no secrets anymore."

With a big, wet sniff: "Riiiight."

Though her voice remained calm, she was crying now in earnest, her cheeks wet and flushed, the water still coming. She cried and she sat, knees akimbo, as if shell-shocked, and he did her the favor of looking straight ahead. In fact, he was glad she had tears left to shed, a body with all its systems active. Crying was at least alive. She heaved, gasped, sobbed.

After a few moments, Christine pressed the sleeve of her spattered smock to her eyes, saying softly through the muffle, "I'm sorry."

Taking her words as permission to again address her, "Why the fuck are you apologizing to me?" he replied, pulling his chin into his neck in incredulity, literally taken aback. However, the curse word elicited a weak smile from Christine. "I'm the one who's sorry," he continued. "I wasn't listening."

"Oh, I wasn't talking," she said, her voice now a clear whisper. "But I didn't know. You know? I've felt this way before, but... I couldn't tell if I was serious, if it was real, and there was only one way to find out. And it seemed welcome, if that makes sense. Putting down a burden, or like taking out an ill-fitting piece of the puzzle, like I never really was meant for the world."

Shifting, Verbenk grabbed his seat and hopped his chair 90 degrees toward her and sat again, leaning forward. The movement made the drop cloth on the floor crunch. And he suddenly understood the plastic, the single chair placed upon it, the purpose of the scene. The drop cloth was to have been her janitor's bucket, her way of preventing discourteous mess. She was going to sit in this chair his ass was occupying and...

No. This time was not that one. That was never going to happen again.

"You were serious enough," he said, tapping his foot on the plastic.

Christine's face collapsed and she let her head fall toward him so their bowed heads rested only inches apart. Even her chin was wet. Her hair lit like a mane as the sun came out through the glass behind her. Instinctively, without thought to consequences and without dwelling on memories of other touched patients—skirts on floor and footless shoes—Verbenk took one of her hands in both of his.

And Christine let him, her fingers returning his pressure.

"And you thought that if you did this," he prompted, "then...?"

"It would serve Dave right somehow?" she asked. "That sounds so juvenile, I know, but also there's a certain symmetry. My art has always been my truth, and that I'd become it?"

He squeezed her hand in response.

Tears still coated her cheeks. "So what happens now?" she asked, her voice small and fearful, obviously thinking of nurses and suicide watches and inpatient programs and urgent conversations over the Atlantic that revealed her tender secrets. He saw a picture of Christine committed, wearing the same pattern of gown his mother had.

Fuck, no. He would not take her there, not if he could help it.

In a whisper, she continued, "What do I do now?"

"You mean, what do we do now," he replied.

The phone, now in his back pocket, vibrated, but of course he could not, would not, let go of Christine's hands now. The only thing that was important was her safety— and he had the best and most covert suicide watcher of all on his team. Rather than remove Christine from everything familiar at this stressful moment, he closed his eyes and concentrated on his question for Janet.

Verbenk strained—the closest to prayer he'd ever been in his life—and asked her to text again him if she agreed with his forming plan. To send no message if he was wrong that she was past the danger. To text if Christine would be OK for the short term.

After a beat, a buzz of affirmation from his pants, and he took a deep breath of relief. Christine was alive and was going to stay that way—at least for the moment, *wanted* to stay that way. He, too, was alive and now felt it more than ever, more than he had in years.

Thank you, he effused toward Janet, *from the both of us.*

"Well," said Verbenk, still careful, keeping his voice calm and nonthreatening, "as for next steps, there are some pharmaceutical options to talk about eventually, but perhaps not right this moment. First, we're going to call your son, OK? We're going to tell him to bring back...?" He fumbled yet again for the wolfhound's name.

She sniffed. "Georgia?"

"Right." Verbenk smiled and squeezed her hand. "Georgia. Eric—with Georgia, of course—is going to spend the night here with you, OK? At least one night, just for company, not as a babysitter or anything. Tell him whatever you want. That you don't feel well. That you're having a hard time and need him. That you have a new painting to show him."

Her smile flickered again.

"Tomorrow, we'll get you a new doctor, too. Someone you *do* feel comfortable talking to, now that we're just neighbors and all," he said, raising a hand to stop her tearful objection. "No, no. We'll start there, shall we? In the meantime, until he arrives," he added, leaning back and let go her hand, knowing that sometimes stories were the best medicine of all. "Have you ever seen *Buffy the Vampire Slayer*?"

Forehead wrinkled, taken aback, Christine sputtered, "Wh... Huh? Really? Who are you today?"

"Oh, I'm full of surprises," he said, slapping his palms on his bare knees in readiness. "It's really quite good. All about fighting demons—" He winked at his patient, whose eyes were finally opening again beyond a slit, like an animal newly born. "—which you know something about, right?"

She snorted and tossed her ponytail. "I suppose I do."

As Verbenk regained his feet, ready to help Christine back into the main house, outside the sunroom he saw a hand appear above the Blum's back fence, obviously on the end of a stretching arm. It bounced up and down as Janet leapt, giving him a gleefully victorious thumbs up.

7

"I don't want to," Verbenk complained, ambling to a halt. A cramp in his right flank threatened to crunch his body in half at the waist and further constrict his straining lungs.

"We're taking a light jog here, not marathoning, and our adventure yesterday only proves you need to be in better shape," Janet said as she bounced in place in tight leggings, dancing on the balls of her sneakered feet. "How long has it been since you worked out? And no." She clapped her hands, as if preventatively dismissing nonsense. "Masturbation is not exercise."

"So say you," the doctor huffed. With his hands on his knees, Verbenk's locked elbows seemed to be the only thing holding him upright—other than what pride he had left in front of this telepath, which was refreshingly minimal. "I'll have you know I lettered in varsity mastur-bation in high school."

Janet cocked her head, still jogging in place, and then smiled, bemused. "And for chess club. Nerd. Now let's move."

Not yet caffeinated, Verbenk resented her bright-eyed humor. Even her leggings were too perky: a thigh-sucking pattern of hot-pink leopard. He pictured kicking her, his sneaker print on her spotted butt in his mind. The thought earned him only more side-eyed bemusement.

Unlike his mind, his body nonetheless obeyed her com-mand, stumbling on in discomfort beside her along the Wash Park jogging path, which was now oh-so familiar. It had been clear when she dragged him out of his house this morning—"A different kind of training!" she'd said— that 'no' was not an acceptable answer. If he'd thought Janet when angry was a force to be reckoned with, well, he was quickly discovering that Janet's enthusiasm was even more in-fucking-vincible. The woman seemed to go up to 11 in all things.

"And why not be enthusiastic?" she asked. "Take in this morning, my friend, so full of possibility."

The doctor watched jealously as she deeply inhaled the air of autumn in Colorado, crisp and clean, while he struggled for breath. In order to match his plodding pace, she still hopped from foot to foot, taking what must have been double his steps. Now she gestured to the park's lake to their left, birds not yet flown south tracing lazy circles on the water—above her sunken keys and belongings.

Opening her arms wide, she said, "It's a beautiful day in a beautiful place, and we have exciting things to discuss. The possibilities!"

"Possibilities?" Verbenk gasped.

"Yeah," said Janet. "I mean, after yesterday."

Oh. Yesterday. Indeed. Today, everything for Janet was about yesterday, but Verbenk, on the other hand, wasn't quite sure what to think about yesterday's adventure. He supposed he hadn't yet had time to process the experience. After their Cyrano-style intervention, he'd returned home, stumbled upstairs to his bed for the first time in a week, and slept deeply, waking with a loafer still on one foot and the other lost in the bedsheets.

Frankly, he also just didn't want to "process the experience," in his field's words, because today he felt... good? It had been a long time, and the mood was rusty, but yes. He felt *good*, and the emotion was so fragile and unfamiliar that he was afraid to look at it head-on lest the frog stop dancing.

"We have to get you in better shape, because doing this jogging-buddies thing for real is the perfect plan," Janet streamed on as they climbed a slight rise in the path that might as well have been a mountain. "It gives us a reason for a relationship, you know? Running like this can be our *cover*."

Obviously pleased with herself, she winked at him over the word cover and grinned. All the way to the park in the car—her driver was waiting in the parking lot, probably squeezing, releasing, squeezing, releasing, the poor fellow—Janet had been bubbling over with all things *yesterday*. Every detail rehashed through her exclamations of: "Remember when I...?" and "But I can't believe you..." and "Weren't we brilliant? Really. Weren't we brilliant?"

And now cover?

While Verbenk was thrilled to sit back in the glow of a satisfactory conclusion to an almost impossible situation, Janet had already started making plans, having gotten the idea in her head that yesterday had been the beginning of something. She'd latched onto the ridiculous fantasy that the two of them, doctor and politician, were going to repeat their strange adventure. That they were going into some superheroing together.

Which, come on now. They save one life—if you could even say that, because even Christine didn't know what she'd been capable of. Still, they save one life—even if by pure trial-and-error luck—and suddenly they're a crime-fighting duo with a need for *cover*. Hilarious, given how she'd previously dismissed his comic-book-driven ideas as comical, but Verbenk had read enough of the genre to know that superheroing involved secret missions, mortal danger, spandex outfits, building-jumping, lots and lots of running, and did he already say mortal danger?

"No," he said. "Not gonna happen."

"Oh, we'll see about that," Janet replied.

Then suddenly, she held out a hand to stop Verbenk where the pedestrian path crossed the road looping around the park. Out of nowhere, a group of men on bikes with what seemed like paper-thin frames flew by them like a cloud burst.

"Wait," she added, still holding out her roadblock, her other hand pressed at her temple. A straggling racer in a red helmet and wrap-around glasses popped out from what seemed like nowhere to catch up to his friends.

"Thanks for saving me that emergency-room visit," said Verbenk, who barely had breath to speak, let alone brainpower to concentrate on anything outside of moving his bodyweight forward. Jogging felt like steering a flesh-mobile of jello. In his current state, he probably would have walked unwitting into the jaws of death—and would do so willingly if this jogging session went past the 30-minute mark. Telepathy to his rescue. Yet again.

Janet again began to jog forward at his pace, still bouncing, bouncing, bouncing extra steps. She swallowed hard and pulled a face. "The headache on that biker was monstrous. I could taste it. But he got himself here this morning anyway, so good for him."

The park was busy this early, much more so than their last visit. Mostly full parking lots, panting dogs on leashes, some kind of outdoor bootcamp-y workout group high-knee kicking through an obstacle course up on the soccer field. To willingly subject herself to so many other people—not just willingly, but without much visible distress—Janet must have been feeling strong indeed.

The opposite of him, then. He was weak and old and wheezy.

A woman with a jogging stroller appeared from around a corner in front of them, motoring their way. The runner, fresh-faced and pretty, passed with a polite nod to Janet—who cheerily waved back—and a side eye for Verbenk.

He must look a fright. His face felt hot enough to toast bread and was likely his least favorite shade: mottled.

"That one's trying to lose the baby weight," Janet whispered, though the woman had looked athletic enough to the doctor. Women worried way too much about appearance shit, he was coming to realize, more than he believed anyone looking at them really cared. So much wasted mental energy. No wonder world peace was still out of reach.

Verbenk snorted in amusement at his own wit, then went back to concentrating on putting one foot in front of the other. He slowed down to wipe his sweaty forehead with the tail of his T-shirt, exposing his belly and the yellowing waistband of his 30-year-old gym shorts, but he had no energy to care, all of it wrapped up in continuing this torturous forward momentum.

Janet's head tilted like an antenna. Honing in the ability, he thought. Wielding it now with skill and confidence—but now toward... him? She listened hard for a moment, only to say in either surprise or disappointment, "Huh."

"What?" he demanded, because his muscles were toast and he was cranky. "What did I do now?"

"You just let a hot woman's ass pass un-fantasized," she said, and winked. "I guess exercise can clean up even the dirtiest mind."

Verbenk pulled back, his face scrunching in horror. "Never! Brains just act strangely when they're *strangled* and *dying.*"

Fuck it. He needed a rest and didn't care if he had permission from his "jogging buddy." Thankfully there was a bench within a dozen paces to collapse upon. In front of him, like a parade, the wider road around the park was as busy as a gym with bikers and the occasional throw-back rollerblader—all whooshing on by with enviable lack of visible effort. When he was already feeling pain in every joint below the waist.

Assholes, he thought, though he found it difficult to muster his normal, lashing bile.

"Oh, stop." Janet hopped foot to foot while he rested, running her miles in place, not a strand of her strawberry-blond escaped from behind her headband. "Your pain's nothing," she said, indicating a group of power walkers with child-sized dumbbells in their hands. "That woman there—" She must have been 80, brittle bones held together by a track suit. "—had knee-replacement surgery six weeks ago, it hurts like hell, and she's moving faster than you."

He grimaced in second-hand—or rather, third-hand—pain. "Well, aren't you happily up in everyone's business today?" asked Verbenk, again amazed at her calm. "Up in everyone's minds?"

Here they stood, within stone's throw distance of their experiment, during which he'd sat on a bench identical to this one and, like a father with his child in the deep end of the pool, he'd nervously watched as Janet probed tentatively, searching for subjects. Back then, people were horrible, *horrible*, and him chief among them. But today, Janet seemed unflappable. A small wince here and there of reaction to overheard thoughts. The clench of a fist on the way to the park. A hitched breath. Signs of distress that likely only he could see.

"You're getting better at this power thing, you know," he said.

"I've..." She hesitated, blushing, itched her nose and looked away, still jogging in place. "I've been practicing. While you were hibernating, I..." Janet paused to let a jogger pass before she continued, despite the woman's head-phoned obliviousness. "I kept up the immersion therapy. You were right." She bit her lip, the admission obviously painful. "It gets easier with practice."

"Ha!" he ejected, bubbling with happiness and clapping his hands on his knees. "I did that! Don't you forget it."

"Only if you don't let it go to your head," countered Janet, who he now pictured doing immersion therapy at that yoga class she tried, wondering what else she might have gotten up to. Without verbalizing the question, she answered with pride, her chin lifted, "I also sat in Star-bucks, just letting the people wash over me until I couldn't take it anymore. I'm up to fifteen minutes now. And yeah, that stuff helped, but was nothing compared to yesterday. It's all about yesterday."

Verbenk groaned.

Without rancor, "Don't dismiss this, asshole," she said, the name almost but not quite a term of endearment.

"Helping Christine was a high, you know? A physical high. There was this moment of..." She held out her hand as if it gripped an invisible ball, searching for the right name for the magic.

The magic he'd also felt. He and Christine, so separated by personality and position (and attractiveness), had been talking past each other, drifting around the world like magnets of the same charge, forcefielded. During their intervention the previous day, the urgency of the situation had definitely contributed, forcing him into action instead of overthink, but the real catalyst to breakthrough had been Janet. Or rather, the bridge of Janet, which had somehow flipped those magnets around to face one another and click.

Connection. He fucking loved that click.

Her eyes widened in passionate agreement. "Yes. Connection. That's it exactly," said Janet, now talking with her hands. "You put your shit aside because someone else was more important. I watched you strip away your acting and your fear—you are normally so careful and conscious—"

Verbenk leaned back into the wooden slats, recognizing himself in her words. He wasn't surprised at this point by her power or her keen intelligence, but hearing his inner life described in such clear and, frankly, *normal* language was enlightening. How long had his defenses been so carapace-thick? How long had he been faking it, faking everything?

"—And I listened thunderstruck as you spread all that plentiful bullshit for her to see, your most tender secrets," she streamed on, "until you were just a flawed, fucked-up ball of raw humanity, steaming and—"

"Hey, now," he objected, because there was such a thing as too far.

"No," said Janet, holding up a finger. "Don't even be embarrassed, because that's what did it, isn't it? You created this human connection that was…" For a moment, she stopped jogging, standing still and speaking clearly—as if she expected him to misconstrue her words and wanted no mistake: "It was beautiful. Really."

The doctor flushed. "Messy, though," he felt it necessary to add. The cut offs, his unbrushed teeth and wild hair, his unplanned sharing. Laying his tender firing on the dissection table for other eyes to pick apart, which is perhaps why the event seemed finally dead to him. Behind him.

"Messy, sure, but also beautiful and human and *essential* in way that—I admit—I've never even attempted to be with most people," said Janet, bouncing back up to speed, a woman of action. Her cheeks were pink, brimming with health.

"So yesterday," she continued, fully in public speaker mode, her voice clear and confident. "Yesterday: *That* was helping people. That was purpose. Small scale, personal, tangible helping." She hit one fist against the other palm with each word. "And none of it needed influence or political compromise or fucking fundraising. Yesterday makes $125,000—even a million—seem cold and impersonal in comparison, doesn't it?"

"Hey," he interjected, sitting up straight. "Don't doubt the big difference you've made for that organization and for the refugee cause in gen—"

"I'm not! I'm not," said Janet, brushing off the thought with a flick of her fingers. "What I mean is that, hey, fuck this refugee-adoption bill that Orin *isn't* going to introduce today as planned."

"Oh, is Orin back in—?"

"Yes. Or he was here last night for an event." She tersely nodded, the subject obviously ground she didn't want to cover just now. An old issue. A pre-yesterday problem. "He's heading back to D.C. this morning. Fly in and fly out. He..." A sigh of contained frustration. "He hasn't figured out how to tell me that the bill is definitely not going to happen. He's breaking up the exploratory committee today. He's going to try to deliver the news when we talk tonight. On the phone. Like a coward."

Verbenk pressed his lips together. "I'm sor—"

Janet snapped, "Well, I'm not. Seriously, fuck D.C. politics. I have a new idea." She tightened her ponytail, then kicked his sneaker with hers. "So enough rest. You're ready, so let's go, good doctor."

He complied without complaint, hiking up his gym shorts and returning to his plod, progressing sneaker-print by sneakerprint along the asphalt path, occasionally crunching a fallen leaf. Tree branches overhead shook their remaining burdens like rattles, like a drumroll, but Janet's words were still reverberating in his head.

She'd just said "good," hadn't she? Yes. She'd said, "good doctor." *Good* practice, *good* man. Could it be possible? Him?

Janet chose not answer the unspoken question, instead saying, "Don't change the subject back to your nasty past. I dragged you here this morning because I want to make this—" She indicated the bond between them, doctor and patient. "—whatever this is, about other people for once. I think we've both been holding our own shit a little too precious, no? It's time to act."

Oh, he'd certainly let his own pain blind him. The doctor swallowed, seeing the conversational opening he'd been waiting for.

"Speaking... of..." Verbenk struggled to talk at the same time his body was moving. He was aware that the arms were supposed to be part of good running form, but not knowing what to do with them, he glued his elbows to his ribs and felt as ridiculous as a T-rex. "I wanted to—"

Janet immediately began shaking her head. "You don't have to—"

"But I do," he huffed out, because he'd had his head up his ass, a shitty perspective, and telepathic transmission wasn't enough with something this important. Important enough that she'd climbed his fucking fence, after all. Yesterday Janet said she'd come initially to his house because she wanted to hear it, and so he said aloud, with no angst or reservations, "I'm sorry. I'm really sorry. For all the—"

"No. No." She turned around to face him, jogging in reverse with what looked like as much skill as she did forward. "*I'm* sorry, too. I'm so sorry. I had no right to say—"

He flapped a dinosaur arm to silence her. Their eyes met directly and openly, held for a moment of acceptance—*click*—then split apart. That was enough, and enough was huge.

As he struggled onward, panting, Verbenk realized that to an outsider, they must have made a funny picture: a young woman talking energetically to an out-of-shape, balding man who rarely got a word in edgewise. He, however, had rarely had a more open and balanced conversation.

Here in the public sunshine, unfamiliar feelings of levity stripped decades of his cynicism away, letting in the fresh air. All of a sudden—but built up over all these weeks— something inside him had been given away and something filled. He felt known. He felt imperfect but whole, and life seemed, well, possible. Not easy, perhaps, but possible.

As they more closely approached the border of the park, the path began to run parallel to the street and the scene grew even more crowded. Two commuters on bikes—office pants rolled up on the chain-side leg to keep tidy—came flying by in the nearby street's bike lane. Up ahead was a well populated bus stop with a glass shelter where a few commuters waited in a flock of fall outerwear. Too cool to wait with the adults, a handful of kids in hoodies and shorts with bulky backpacks chatted with animated hand gestures.

So many people. So much chaos. Verbenk looked to Janet, who it seemed to him was showing off, being reckless with her own safety. Was courting the mortal danger that frightened him.

She looked back at him and nodded acknowledgment, more than aware of his worry but not seeming phased— although her jog no longer seemed so buoyant. He could hear the regular puffs of her breath now, and at least gravity seemed to again apply to her gait. They were two thirds of the way through one loop, and his quadriceps and calves were protesting. The path was going to ramp back uphill around the corner, he knew, where it curved around to head back north.

"So about this idea of mine," said Janet as they clomped now shoulder to shoulder. "I know how your practice is *thriving* and all, but how do you feel about being Mental Health Liaison for the Denver branch of Love International?" Verbenk did a double-take, missed a step, then scrambled back up to speed as she went on without a pause, "Because as of today, you're officially a Mental Health Liaison for the Denver branch of Love International. I made a call, made it happen. You can sign the papers in the car."

Verbenk looked at Janet's profile, squinted, computed. "I... I don't know what that means."

Breaking into a grin, "It means small-scale superheroing, that person-to-person change, doc," she said. "It means that I, the organization's chair, am putting away the evening gown and going into the field. Finally. Tomorrow

I'm meeting with a Congolese woman, a single mother with two young daughters, to help the family move into their first American apartment. You know, help them sort the donated furniture, find the nearest bus stop, give them a key to a door after more than four years in a refugee camp. That kind of thing."

The Congo, thought Verbenk. His mind went to news footage of young men in army green uniforms and bandoliers of bullets, of reports of child soldiers and rape being used as a weapon of war. A single mother with two girls... Despite the warmth of the day, he shivered.

"Yes. Lots of trauma there." Janet paused to swallow, pushing down emotion, struggling for words. "It's going to be..."

"Messy?" he supplied.

"And..."

"Difficult?"

"Yeah."

"And you're going to do wonderful," said Verbenk with utter sincerity, more than a little impressed. "Good for you."

Good, good, good. Good was blooming like dandelions today, those same hardy weed-flowers which were sprouting through the seams of the path they chugged along. Delicate flowers that, given time and space, could bust through concrete.

"You mean," said Janet as she turned her head toward him, testing the waters, biting her lip, "good for *us*, right? That *we* are going to be wonderful? Because without you

there, as well, I can't do... I can't go and—I mean especially with their history, I just..."

Verbenk nodded through her anxiety. Mental Health
Liaison, huh? Stupid title, that, but there was little point in
disagreement or even in jokey mental complaining about
this twist Janet had designed for him. He was going to do
it, the doctor discovered in surprise. There was no question: If Janet was going to hero, he would be her sidekick.

He could see the cover of the comic now: Telepath Girl...
Telepath Woman and Dr. Shrink! He'd do whatever Janet
needed, because this painful goose-chase of a therapeutic journey had felt like destiny throughout. And besides,
he thought with determination, he had a lot of amends to
make, and being the man who stood behind this storm of
a woman, fueling her fight, was a great place to start.

Janet reached over to pat Verbenk's back, but thankfully withdrew in time—most likely because she could feel
his stinky, free-flowing sweat. Or rather, she could feel
him feeling the sweat run down his back. Poor woman.
Even he hated that feeling, and Janet had to share it.

She settled instead for a touched smile and a deliberate
head nod, the kind male athletes gave one another instead
of hugs, and said, "Thanks, Dr. Shrink."

He laughed two quick syllables, but then suddenly,
Janet was no longer beside him. She just disappeared, as if
he'd sprinted away from the pack, though his pace hadn't
changed and gods knew that the concept of sprinting was
purely aspirational for Verbenk at this point.

Stopping, turning, fists still primed, he saw Janet 10 feet behind him, frozen, like a dropped juggling ball. All color had drained from her face and she'd turned to look back south, staring. Janet pressed her temple with one hand and her stomach with the other. She was now the one hyperventilating.

"What?" Verbenk snapped, stepping forward and reaching for her shoulder. His eyes darted left and right, scanning like radar for the possible source of her telepathic distress. The bus stop on Downing Street was a stone's throw away along the sidewalk behind him, a traffic light a few feet further on. "Too many people? See? Just as I—"

"No," she said, her tone cutting through any possible levity or told-you-so's. "Is this—? Ow! Can't be a heart attack, can it? Fuck, ow!"

"What?" demanded Verbenk. "Who?!"

"I'm trying," she muttered, head cocked at an extreme angle, eyes unfocused.

But the scene was now too busy for him to pinpoint anything. Cars and SUVs rolled by in both directions. A dog pulling on a leash barked emphatically, brakes squeaked, the pack of middle schoolers in boxy backpacks at the bus stop burst into in-joke laughter.

"She's— ouch!" Janet pushed out, obviously in pain, which pressed her eyebrows together and collapsed her face. She clutched her chest again, then bolted upright, as if electrocuted. "I think she's… seizing now? She's not going to be able to stop!"

The doctor went for her hand, but Janet's wrist slipped through his fingers as she took off at a run down the path they'd just traveled. Frantic, he too looked south: Among the moderate traffic, a city RTD bus stood out on the narrow one-lane street like a tall man in a crowd, about half a block away with the traffic light between them. He heard several bursts of air brakes and the noise of a revving commercial engine.

"Move!" a running Janet shouted toward the people on the sidewalk, waving her arms, her gaze flicking back and forth between them and the bus. The source was definitely the bus. That's what wasn't going to be able to stop. "Move back! Run!"

At the shelter, a woman in blue scrubs and a wrinkled, elderly man with a puffy jacket turned, as did one of the kids, pointing to his friends and laughing at the crazy adult.

"Move back!" Janet repeated, seeming to shout now toward pedestrians on the opposite side of the street, her hand cupped around her mouth.

Already in motion in Janet's wake, Verbenk watched the bus in fear. Sun glinted off its wide windshield, but he could see motion inside the cabin. Then the bus suddenly jerked to the right and the left, the latter swinging the wheels over the double-yellow mid line of the street before the behemoth yanked back into its lane. Luckily the other side of the narrow street was empty. But the light was red ahead of it, and the bus would be expected to stop.

A chill ran down Verbenk's spine and into his sneakers, and time began to run slowly, like a snapping, 35mm classroom film, played at half speed.

"Ruuuun!" said Janet, though her voice was now strangled. One hand clutched at her chest and the other at her throat, the fingers clawed, as if she were strangling.

All eyes at the bus stop were on her now, this strange woman, having a kind of fit. The kids were all pointing. The woman in scrubs exclaimed something and began to run to meet Janet, several others straggling behind her.

Janet choked, couldn't seem to draw breath.

Finding energy he would have sworn he didn't possess, Verbenk was somehow one step behind her as she stumbled, but kept her feet. Then her eyes rolled upward into her head, exposing the vulnerable whites. Another seemingly drunken step, her ankle turned, and she went down, the fabric of her shirt slipping from between his reaching fingers.

Her head made a sickening thwack against the curb where path met grass. Her eyes were closed, her mouth still open and Verbenk howled.

"Dayum!" said a young voice.

Verbenk looked up to see the middle-school leader, trailing a pack of his friends. The scrubbed woman asked, "Is she all right?" All of them now standing safely away from the street—as Janet intended, he realized. Like she'd taken his ledge-leaper and baby-carriage saving talk as a challenge.

Just then: air brakes, a squeal of tires, the noise of shifting sheets of metal. Amid a flurry of honks, the bus sailed through the nearby intersection, almost clipping a motorcyclist, who swerved up onto a lawn to avoid a crash. Horns sounded, one car crunched into the fender of another, yet the dumb rectangle of death continued on, listing to the right.

Janet became secondary to everyone else's worries when the bus crested the park-side curb with two wheels and people screamed.

But she wasn't secondary to Verbenk. Flinging himself to the ground alongside Janet, scraping his knees, he leaned his ear over her mouth, her warm, moist breathing too shallow. What had she done?

He checked her pulse, which was racing, and her eye dilation. A concussion at least, said his medical experience.

Glancing up, he saw the bus take out a blue newspaper machine, which flew apart at its metal seams and tossed a cloud of today's editions into the air. Two wheels up and two down, it slowed only incrementally as it approached the bus shelter, which was endcapped with an ad of a blonde woman holding an expensive purse.

The dozen people standing in the grass less than a dozen feet away—thanks to Janet—watched slack-jawed. Glass crunched and flew. The blonde seemed to bend at the waist, still smiling, as the bumper of the bus pushed into the shelter and into the bench inside, both of which thankfully worked to slow its momentum. Verbenk heard shouts from inside the bus as it rocked back on its wheels to a stop.

And like a rubber band snapping back, the film of time caught up, then began to run too fast around Verbenk, but he focused only on Janet.

No neck injury, it seemed, but he was nonetheless extremely careful when working his fingertips lightly over her skull. A big egg of swelling. At least one jagged laceration, wet and slippery, small but bleeding as all head wounds do: freely. Blood down her neck and on her headband and matted in her hair. Concussion, easy.

A siren sounded, roaring up around the usually pedestrian and bike-only road around Wash Park, which he now vaguely remembered had a fire station on the far side. The emergency vehicles were on the scene within moments. Male voices of calm command shouted questions, and one said, "You two, the bus. You, check the bystanders."

All the bus-stoppers began to gather around Verbenk and Janet, a tightening circle crowding out their sunlight. *People*. Panicked people. *Fuck*. He had no idea if Janet was still able to absorb their messy, overwhelming minds, but her breath seemed to grow even fainter.

A male voice, "Out of the way unless you're injured, people."

Then arms—clothed in short sleeves of first-responder blue, studded with official ID patches he didn't read—were manhandling Verbenk off Janet, pushing him aside and onto his ass.

"Was she involved in the accident?" the squatting EMT asked. "Sir?"

He couldn't answer. The faces of onlookers loomed, worried and entertained and curious and scared.

"Give her space!" Verbenk shouted at them, pushing himself back to a kneel, doing his best not to panic. He grabbed Janet's hand.

"Sir, you, too. Give her space," said the EMT, who was repeating the same emergency diagnostics Verbenk had just done. He called to his partner, and the man brought a bright-yellow spine board and laid it beside her.

"She'll be at National Jewish, sir, if you'd like to follow," said the first EMT, who ripped Janet's hand away from the doctor. With his partner, the man moved her body onto the board, then six inches up onto the portable gurney, her small sneakers wobbling as they unfolded the wheels and the bed popped up to waist height.

The radio on the EMT's belt squawked: "Multiple minor casualties on the bus. Contusions, whiplash, cuts and bruises. Man, this could have been a lot worse. The bus driver is on board to Jewish, code three."

Pressing the button on his radio, "I have one more code three, bystander, unknown head trauma, unconscious," the EMT shot back.

"Make it two in back as we triage here," said the radio.

National Jewish, Verbenk mentally repeated. The hospital. The very same tower of tragedies that previously had almost run him and Janet off the road.

"No," he whispered. "Nononnononono..."

They were taking Janet from this nightmare toward her worst one.

"Let's go," said the EMT's partner, and before Verbenk could act, they were running with prone Janet toward a nearby ambulance, parked along with a fire truck on either side of the still bus. Other cars were scattered around the street, stuck but safe, and a cop was laying down cones to start traffic diversion.

"I'm coming with! I'm her friend!" Verbenk shouted, back on his feet and sprinting. He loped alongside the gurney, his fingers clutching at the buckles which held Janet in place like a trussed pork roast.

"National Jewish," the man repeated, waving him away. "We're already carrying two."

"I'm also her doctor," insisted Verbenk instead.

The EMT finally looked Verbenk square in the face, efficient brown eyes asking for confirmation of that fact. Verbenk nodded, and after a thoughtful beat, the man said, "Don't get in the way." Verbenk nodded again more frenetically. Janet wasn't going anywhere alone.

The scene streamed onward, words and actions fast as hummingbird wings. The floor of the ambulance rocked beneath Verbenk's feet as he climbed aboard and he found himself in a narrow aisle between two gurneys. The EMT shoved up behind him, pushing Verbenk into the sliver of space between Janet's head and the driver's cabin. Doors slamming. Various beeps and signals.

The EMT worked between Janet's stretcher and that of the other patient in the vehicle: a plump middle-aged woman in a large, beige bra, visible where her transit uniform had been cut down the center. The bus driver. Eyes wide open in panic, she was gasping for air, red-faced, her muscles tense and vibrating. The brown-eyed man worked over her, nonchalantly siding a tube down her protesting throat, asking his partner how long ago epinephrine had been delivered.

"Administering a second dose, then," he said, and pulled an epi pen out of one of many pants pockets.

Not a heart attack, as Janet had suspected. *Anaphylaxis*. Certainly explained the runaway bus. The woman was having an extreme and incredibly frightening—sometimes deadly—allergic reaction. And his telepath was two feet from the nightmare, defenseless and very absorptive.

"ETA two minutes," called the driver.

The EMT worked more frantically, and Verbenk watched as Janet's heart rate—the monitor clamped to her finger—sky rocketed, and he realized it was even worse that he thought. Her blood pressure was falling, blue visibly leeching into her coloring.

Fuck. Even if unconscious, she was definitely absorbing. He grabbed Janet's hand in both of his, encasing it. Still the heart-rate monitor beeped its warning and, closing his eyes, Verbenk tried to breathe. He tried to calm himself, at least, but it was impossible against all the moving pieces.

I'm here, he thought, teeth-clenchingly hard.

"Her oxygen level is falling, too," the EMT muttered, now looking at Janet's read-outs then back and forth between his patients. "Like dominoes. Huh."

More closing car doors. Sunlight shone again into the ambulance bay and firm ground was under his feet. The standard fluorescents and clipped tones of the emergency room, familiar from his long-ago, half-assed residency. Children sobbing, junkies ODing, broken bones and influenza and the garden-variety ailments of the uninsured, who drooped listless and depressed in every chair and corner.

Unconscious, vulnerable Janet in the middle. Her breathing almost undetectable now.

Questions were asked and answered around him, but Verbenk paid no attention, clinging to Janet's bedside even while she was transferred with a team-effort lift onto a hospital cot. Behind a curtain to their right, someone screamed, while around him, quick-fire medical jargon flew back and forth.

"Possible swelling on the brain..."

"... ordered the EEG."

"I'd intubate immediately," said the EMT. "Respiration abnormal."

But Verbenk understood the situation as well as any of them: patient vitals crashing, possible TBI, traumatic brain injury. He'd seen damage occur in more benign-seeming accidents than the blow she'd sustained. They could not know to add, however: currently engulfed in massive amounts of psychic pain with unknown short- and long-term results. What was happening to Telepath Woman?

You didn't perhaps hit your head? echoed his own voice in his mind.

'*What?*' she'd replied. '*You want to hit me on the head again, and it will all go away?*'

"Sir, you'll have to leave now," said a woman with a messy bun and an officious manner, who Verbenk took for either an ER resident or the department's star nurse. Either way, the most competent person in the room.

"No. I'm her private physician," he said.

"Family only in the—"

"I'll make more fuss if you kick me out than if you let me stay," he clipped. "You have better things to do than deal with me."

The young woman—everyone was so fucking young, but they'd better be good—bit her lip, pressed her charts to her chest and sighed. "I do. Everyone's accident prone this morning. We're packed. Sit in that chair and out of the way," she said, pointing, and he held up his hands in obedience. The moment he was out of the medical staff's way, they swarmed the gurney, and he watched as a plastic tube was thrust down her throat to keep the airway open. He almost cried, imagining what she was going through, feeling so very impotent.

"This brain activity is abnormal. Off the charts."

"Wait, she's—"

And Janet began to seize, bucking against the hands of the medical team, gods only knew what was happening in her special, fragile brain. Tears streamed unheeded down his face. He must have made to stand.

"Chair!" the nurse yelled at him, pointing without turning. Eyes in the back of her head.

Falling into the chair in obedience, Verbenk did the only thing he could for Janet now: create safety. Eyelids pressed closed, he slammed all his own emotions into a mental closet, tuned out every distraction and focused.

Breathe the tide in. Breathe the tide out.

An emergency code was announced on the hospital's paging system. A herd of orthopedic shoes outside the curtains headed toward a different crisis, while his own set of medical professionals continued their flurry.

"No signs of cardiac distress."

"Why the hell isn't she breathing?!"

Grasping the armrests of the plastic chair with white-knuckled determination, Verbenk dove deeper into the guided meditation. Despite the stress, this time the ocean came without complaint, cool and refreshing, shushing up the beach and then back out, pulling sand grains from between his toes.

Breathe in the tide, breathe the chaos out. I'm here, Janet. I'm here.

The world swirled on around them, but there on the beach in his mind, Verbenk saw two children, bodies still round with the remnants of babyhood. A boy and a girl, the latter with strawberry-blond pigtails, wet at the ends from swimming. Together, they built a sandcastle with their plastic buckets and plastic spades. The sun warmed their shoulders, the smell of sunscreen and salt. Together, they made a tower at each corner and dug a moat, even decorated the sand edifice with found seashells like some fantasy Kodak moment, and it *was* perfect. Further up the beach, keeping the distance of the dead, was his mom, her legs crossed on a towel, waving happily.

As if from far away, Verbenk heard the beeping of Janet's monitors begin to slow and the voice of the woman said, "I'll be damned. She's stabilizing."

Breathe in the tide, let go the pain.

"We'll need to assess Glasgow..."

"Schedule MRI."

"Doctor?" the competent woman's voice asked Verbenk, close in front of him, but the doctor would not open his eyes. "Sir, she's... Are you OK?"

Clenching his eyes further shut, he nodded.

Verbenk could feel her continued presence, hovering. "Sir?"

"I'm fine," he snapped. "Let me be, right here."

At that point, she or someone else pressed disinfectant-cold cotton ball to his knees and stuck on Band-Aids, muttering, but only the ocean mattered. Two kids on a beach playing to the soundtrack of Janet's regularly beeping heart.

Despite her new calm, he continued the guided meditation for the sake of her brain—if it were still whole, still special. If the ability could come, it could also go, right? And rather than being relieved that she might no longer have that psychic burden that had caused her so much pain, Verbenk was terrified. He'd made room on the beach. Now he didn't know if he could inhabit it alone.

He didn't know if he could live without this strange friendship. He didn't know if he'd still be the changed man he was with Janet when without her.

Verbenk didn't know how long he meditated at her side, but he must have concentrated himself into oblivion and then unwilling sleep because he woke with a start. His fingers were stiff and sore from holding onto the chair. As he brought his head up, he could feel the indentation on the side of his forehead where his face had fallen against her bed frame. His hamstrings had tightened like guitar strings, and he remembered he'd been foolishly exercising.

"I said, who are you?" a man asked, urgently, jostling Verbenk's shoulder. The man, Verbenk decided, who must have woken him.

The doctor turned his blurry head and found the man in question was: Senator Orin Buckmann. Dark hair peppered with just a touch of rich silver, aged 45. Bright blue (babe-magnet) eyes, which matched the blue stripes in his tie, stripes which lined up perfectly between tie and knot. And that chin. A very distinguished cleft chin, almost Disney in design.

Verbenk felt star struck, as if a fictional character had come to life and was standing before him.

Obviously upset, "Well?" Buckmann demanded.

"I'm... Derek. I was there, at the park," he replied, stuttering and nervous, attempting to sit up straight despite the cricks in his back. "Janet and I are..." He stumbled for words. "...jogging buddies." She was right. The excuse was handy.

"Well, thank you for being here with her," he said, his face relaxing from panic to skepticism. Verbenk only now noticed the smart phone in the man's hand, which he shook by way of excuse. "Can you sit with her one moment more, buddy? I'm supposed to be somewhere else right now. Thanks."

Orin spun around and began talking, pacing in a small circle just outside the opened patient curtains, and Verbenk looked at Janet.

"I know," the Senator said to his unseen minion. "Yes. I know!" Then softer, "But it was a pointless meeting anyway. Thank everyone for their work, of course, but... No, I can't make promises at this point."

Though an oxygen cannula was slotted into Janet's nostrils, the intubation was removed. Unlike the last time the doctor had seen her, her face was calm and peaceful— as if she, too, just had a pleasant dream—despite the obvious white bandage behind her ear. There was no way to know what was going on in her head, if she was OK in there. What if she woke up different? What if the last two weeks were erased from her memory along with her power and she no longer knew him?

Without fanfare or self-pity, Verbenk silently cried, a few hot tears wetting each cheek.

"Absolutely not. I'll catch a later flight, Greg, as soon as I can, but I have to tell her myself," Orin was saying, intermittently visible through the crack of the curtains while he paced, running his fingers through his hair. "It's a serious concussion, even if they say she'll make a full recovery."

The doctor melted in relief at this news. A full recovery!

"No. Well... Blame *this* for canceling?" Orin glanced back at his wife, then stepped farther into the hall. "You really think her accident in the media could give me a boost? Man, I don't know."

"Ugh," Verbenk gagged softly, choking on moral compromise. He looked to Janet, wanting to trade an eye roll of shared distaste, but she hadn't moved, so small and lifeless in her bed, a puppet without animating personality.

But just then, one of Janet's fingers twitched. Her cheeks were flushed and pinking. Her eyes flickered, then opened. Verbenk drew closer as she tried and failed to talk, her throat likely tender and bruised.

Weakly, she pointed toward Orin with a finger lifted only an inch. She tried to speak, but it seemed too much effort. She was exhausted and her lips were dry, even cracked.

"Greg, I know," Orin was saying. "Tell him I hold him in the highest of respect and regard, all that shit, and then..."

"What? What do you...?" Verbenk began to say, but Janet pointed again, determined.

You want Orin? he transmitted.

She nodded, but then licked her dry lips again, eyes pleading. Also in that line of pointing was a water pitcher one of the staff must have left on her wheeled, bedside table.

You want water?

A stronger nod of relief, and Verbenk felt a similar cooling suffuse his chest, loosening his old, cranky arteries. Janet was back. She was whole, she was thirsty, and she could still hear him. He half stood from his chair, poured a cup of water for her and called, "Ori—" He stopped himself. "Senator. She's awake. She's asking for you."

The man's handsome head popped back through the curtain, his fingers over the phone's mic. "Babe?" he asked, anxious. The anxiety of his world ending. In those nervous handsome eyes, Verbenk saw the truth of what Janet had told him. Saw the heart behind the tie. Oh, yes. Orin loved her and that love was his saving grace, in the doctor's eyes. "Janet? Babe?"

She managed a smile, and Verbenk put the cup within her reach, sat back in the old visitor's chair and scooted it back to give them privacy as much the curtained room could offer.

Orin rushed to the bed, took her hand in both of his, and held it close to his double-breasted heart. "Thank God," he said. "I don't know what I'd do if—"

"I know," she croaked, and attempted another smile. "But you. You're supposed to be..." She swallowed painfully.

"I'm needed *here*," Orin insisted.

"No," she said, pulling away her hand, pushing herself up onto an elbow and reaching for the water. "No, you have to go to that meeting. Push it back, reschedule, but go. Do like Greg says and use the excuse of this—" As Janet drank, she indicated the hospital around them. "—if you think it will play. I don't care."

The Senator's eyebrows furrowed, his mouth falling open, and he blushed in well-deserved shame. "You heard that just now? Sorry. His idea, not mine. I would *never* without your—"

Janet cleared her throat. "I know, I know, but Martin is going to co-sponsor the refugee bill. I swear, you can make it happen."

Looking once at Verbenk—the doctor immediately pretended his attention was riveted on the scuffed linoleum floor—Orin lowered his voice to more confidential levels and said, "Babe, you don't know what you're talking about."

"Oh, but I do," she said, nodding. "Tell her I know about Nora. Tell her to do it for Nora."

Eyebrows furrowed, "Who—?"

"Doesn't matter," she croaked, then cleared her bruised throat again. "Nora. She'll understand, and I think you can get Villabrand, too. Use his mother to reach him. She escaped Europe in the late 30s and—"

"Janet, you're loopy on drugs or something," said Orin. "You're being naive."

Pointing at him with maternal scolding, "No, I'm being idealistic, and I'm giving the bill a chance," she insisted. Orin made to reply, but she silenced him by adding her second hand to their hand sandwich. "Think for a moment. If you had Martin and Villabrand..."

Orin's eyes had glazed over in thought. "Their support *would* give us a shot, certainly, but that addition to the coalition is not enough to turn the tide. We'd surely lose."

Janet plunged on. "But still, you won't forgive yourself if you give up without a fight. I know you. You once said I was your heart." She flickered a smile and the couple tilted their heads together, reminding the doctor of a wedding-day silhouette portrait. Janet whispered, "Well, your heart is telling you that it's better to try and fail than to never fully put yourself out there at all."

Verbenk's own heart swelled in pride, watching Janet's courage bloom, even if her cheeks were still hollow, her eyes still wild and dazed.

"Nora," Janet repeated. "And Villabrand's mom." Orin opened his mouth, likely to express a doubt, and she held up a finger. "No. Re-election is *not* our primary goal. Change is. Now, are we people of conviction or merely words?"

Orin sniffed, nodded unsure, then set his chin in determination and nodded again. "OK," he said, regaining some of his fast-talking energy. "OK, if I'm really going to do this, risk this... Yes, OK, I'll try, every other thing be damned. There's another flight in—" He looked at his big, silver watch.

"Thirty minutes. Yes. Go!" said Janet, pushing him bodily away from her cot. "Call me tonight."

Orin beamed, kissed her on the forehead and spared one sheepish look for Verbenk, mumbling something about thanks and nice meetings. Then the phone was right back to his ear—had this Greg person been live on the line the whole time?—and he was back in character.

"Change of plan," he said down the line. "Tell them I was delayed with my injured wife, but Greg. We're going to fight it out. Yes. Really. A man's allowed to change his mind, isn't he? I know. Now make it happen, and make sure Villabrand is there."

Then the Senator strode out into the ER hallway, planning, scheming, politicking. Verbenk chuckled softly, and Janet kicked at him with her blanket-held foot.

Still hoarse, now spent, she whispered, "Don't worry. I'm going to be fine, doc." Then pausing to swallow, she added, "Once you get me the fuck out of this hospital, that is, we're going to be fine."

ACKNOWLEDGMENTS

"Transference" would not exist today without the help of my writing family and fellow misfit toys, my critique groups. Thanks to the Alfalfa's (and beyond!) crew: Jane, Marc and Phebe. Also to the epic 30th Street Writers: Caitlin, Evan, Ian, Jessica, Julie, Lezly, Maggie, Michael and Rick. Both groups of dear friends have become the voices in my head, so it's a good thing I like you weirdos. Thanks to my varied and eagle-eyed beta readers Jarred, Jenn, Jessica, Jon/Stan and Zach, and to Mark Middleton for lending his talents to my little project. Go Chargers?

Any writer would be remiss to not also include their favorite coffee shops. Thank you to Ozo Coffee on Arapahoe for the best Masala Chai and to Seeds Library Cafe for their surprisingly tasty beet donuts. Thank you, City of Boulder for providing me space to—never—fit in, and apologies to the City of Denver for any minor inaccuracies necessary to further plot.

While the process of writing and publishing this book took less than two years, becoming the writer I needed to be to create it took far longer, and for that I need to thank my most important person, my husband Brooke. I love you more than the library. Thank you for keeping me in your pocket.

Lastly, a potential call to action. According to the United Nations, a record-breaking 65 million people worldwide were displaced from their homes in 2016. If you'd like to see more of these vulnerable people find new lives in our country and in your community, contact your members of Congress and/or support the work of the UNHCR, the United Nations Refugee Agency (www. unhcr.org). In Colorado, three agencies give material, logistical and emotional support to recent refugees:

The International Rescue Committee, or IRC Denver:
www.rescue.org/united-states/denver-co

The African Community Center:
www.acc-den.org

Lutheran Family Services of the Rocky Mountains:
www.lfsrm.org/programs-and-services/refugees